The Way to Murder

A Board Game Café Mystery

Shelley Shearer

Tannhauser Press

Text copyright © 2023 by Shelley Shearer

Published by Tannhauser Press
www.tannhauserpress.com
First Edition

ISBN: 978-1-958321-01-0
Book cover design by The Killion Group
Formatting by fiverr.com/braniac_

To my family, real and chosen.
I couldn't have done this without you.

What is Letterboxing?

Letterboxing is a type of "treasure hunt" activity, primarily done outdoors. Letterboxers hide small, weatherproof containers and post clues on how to find the boxes online. Boxes are left in publicly accessible places such as parks.

A letterbox generally has a logbook for people to stamp in and a rubber stamp. The rubber stamps are often hand-carved.

When the box is found, the letterboxer inks the stamp, puts the image in their logbook, and leaves a stamped image of their personal stamp in the letterbox's logbook.

What to find out more? Try a few boxes in your area?

Letterboxing LbNA http://www.letterboxing.org

Atlasquest at http://www.atlasquest.com

Chapter One

I slowed as I entered the parking lot full of bystanders. The flashing emergency lights of an ambulance are not something you want to see when pulling up to your friend's apartment.

My heart raced. I scanned the people standing around on the grass until I found Trace standing off to the side with one of her pajama-clad neighbors. My heart rate went from panicked to relieved and curious. I smiled, seeing she had taken my advice and dressed for the outdoors. Her shoulder-length blonde hair was up in a ponytail. She wore a soft jersey, short-sleeved shirt, and jeans, which appeared to have never been worn. They probably hadn't. Trace took to skirts the way I took to yoga pants, and she preferred silks to denim.

"Remi, can you believe it?" Trace came up to me as I got out of my Honda. I caught a glimpse of two men loading a body bag into the ambulance in the background. "It was that guy from downstairs."

"The dancer?" I asked.

"No, the one who makes that dish that smells like rotten fish."

I looked at her, waiting for more information. She wasn't distraught, so I knew it wasn't someone she knew well.

"Remember? The odor comes up and goes straight through my sliding glass door. I have three of those odor-eating gel things I line up around the bottom of the door whenever I catch the first hint of it."

"Right. The emergency trip to the store for those candles last month." I looked around, and people were heading back to their apartments now that the body was gone. "Do you know what happened to him?"

She shook her head, both of us staring at the ambulance closing its doors. "They won't tell me anything. But the few times I saw him getting his mail, he seemed like such a young guy. I can't see it being a heart attack or anything. It had to be an accident."

"Heh, yeah. Accidentally murdered." A guy whose beer belly overflowed his striped sleep pants commented as he walked by us.

"Don't listen to him," a lady piped up, "The poor man must have had a bad reaction to something. His face was all swollen up."

Murder? Not a word I wanted to hear. I checked out her neighborhood with a different eye. On the surface, it had always appeared safe. No welcoming committee with cookies when you moved in, but also no fear of going out to your car at night. I perked up, knowing she could get out of this place soon. My surprise came at the perfect time.

"Come on. Unless you need something else from inside, let's head out of here." I reached to pick up her bag.

"I got it." She said, waving me away.

"Don't worry about it." I grabbed for her bag again.

Trace tilted her head to look around me. "Remi, why don't you want me to put my own bag in the trunk?"

"Sheesh. I was trying to be helpful." I ducked my head as I pulled the keys from my pocket. I thought about stalling, but she remained rooted in place. Why did I bother? During our fifteen years of friendship, she'd seen through everything I'd ever tried.

I popped my trunk open. The luggage and sealed boxes I'd packed left enough of a gap to squeeze in her one overnight bag.

I ignored that she was waiting, stuffed her bag in, closed up the trunk, and jumped into the driver's seat. She followed a moment later.

"I feel I'm missing important information on how much I was meant to pack," she grumbled. "I need to make a quick stop at the cafe."

"You're right. We should pack a kitten." I grabbed a scrunchie from the car tray and gathered my unruly black hair off my neck. My car's air conditioning struggled in the lingering humidity of September.

"We're not taking a kitten. My packages haven't been getting to me at the apartment, so I had my hiking boots shipped there and forgot to pack them."

The tennis shoes she wore would have been fine for the minimal hiking in her future, but why argue? Besides, visiting the cat cafe she worked at part-time meant kitten time and a coffee for the road.

By the time we picked up her boots and snuggled furballs, we were only an hour later than our planned time to be on the road. The two-hour drive into rural Virginia zipped by at first as we chatted, but then last night's volunteer shift at the wildlife center caught up with Trace, and she was asleep against the side window. At a traffic light, I took a quick photo of her sleeping, a drool trail visible against the glass. I texted her a brief note: "Bring two kittens to me on Main St., or this goes viral." The text notification wasn't enough to wake her. I let her keep sleeping for the first twenty minutes of being lost.

Balancing my phone in one hand and holding a Diet Coke in the other didn't leave me many hands for navigating the car. Usually, I was a much safer driver, but we were so very lost. I gave up trying to figure it out and nudged Trace awake.

"Remi, there are, like, three roads to choose from and you've been out here four times already helping Alice get things set up. How can you be lost?" Trace asked as I looked for a road sign. Any sign. After knowing me half my life, I couldn't believe she'd even ask that. If it weren't for the magic of the map apps, I would be three states away in New York about now. Either the app was glitching, or no one had been on this little road in a long time, as the map kept telling me I was in the middle of nowhere. Or a lake. It's disconcerting to look down and have your car icon surrounded by blue. The last sign said I was 7 miles from my destination of Irving, Virginia, and that was twenty minutes ago. The irony was not lost on me that I was lost on my way to host an event where people had to my follow directions to find things. I figured we were all pretty doomed.

Trace's phone vibrated. She shut it down and threw it in her purse. "Not today."

"Why not answer? They could have been in front of a computer. With a **map**." I emphasized.

She shrugged. "Number was blocked. Probably someone trying to sell me something. If it was someone I know, they'd leave a message, right?"

I put my drink in the cup holder on top of some crumpled napkins and a candy wrapper. "Wait a minute. Are you still getting weird calls? The ones you said had stopped. How often are you getting them?"

She crossed her arms and looked out the window to her right.

"Don't make me pull this car over." I threatened.

She waved a hand as if brushing it aside. "I'm probably making too much out of the whole thing. Think of it like when we lived in the townhouse and our phone number was one digit away from the local pizzeria. We got calls constantly asking for our daily special. I probably have a number that someone keeps drunk calling or something." She started nervously playing with her hair.

"Have they ever asked for a pizza? Tried to sell you a timeshare?"

"No. There's just silence. Never a hang-up or 'sorry, wrong number'. Silence, and then I end the call." She plucked my phone from my hand and started pushing buttons. "How do you make this thing show you the larger area?"

She was shutting down. There was no point in bugging her to talk about it now, but we both knew I wasn't going to let it drop forever. Between that and the boxes in the trunk, we'd need a girl's night of playing Zombicide to hash things out.

"Oh! Oh!" I pointed at a large Victorian house on the left. "I recognize that house! It had the cutest calico cat sitting out front. All we have to do now is make the next left, pass Don's Diner, and we'll be almost there." I would never be lost if maps put landmarks like a mailbox shaped like a cow or a yard filled with toys.

"Did you say diner?" Trace perked up and rubbed her eyes. The large neon Diner sign peeked out above the trees. "I could go for some pancakes and bacon."

"You ate two hours ago at the cafe."

"Sue me. I have a fast metabolism. And it's bacon." She pointed to the sign on the roof of the building. "And they have the best pies in the county. Pies." She nudged my shoulder. "You know you like a good homemade pie."

I don't know why she kept trying to talk me into it. I had already put my turn signal on. My jeans were snug lately, but what's wrong with being a little fluffy? A little self-care in the form of pie can be balanced out later with walking the trails.

The car lot was packed. Rule of travel: In a small town, always go where the locals go. Some of our best road trip meals have been in places I would have driven by.

Now that I no longer feared being lost and eaten by bears, the thought of some old-fashioned diner pie made my stomach growl. I pulled into the gravel lot and found one empty spot near the back. Walking in, I noticed that the checkerboard floor and red counter stools had seen better days, but the place was packed with customers. There was one open table in the main dining area. My feet didn't stick to the floor, and the food on the plates promised giant services of mouth-watering eating. I smirked at the heads that turned as Trace walked by. My average height and dark hair blended in. She was tall and runway-ready in a room full of people out for a weekday diner breakfast.

I glanced at the menu's specials on the whiteboard as our waiter came by to pour some water.

"The pancake special, please, with a side of bacon," Trace said.

"Same," I said, digging in my purse.

I pulled out a small tin of Sushi Go cards and dealt Trace her stack. Ever since we met, we'd spend our time playing games, eating way too much food, and chugging caffeine. We both had gotten into the habit of carrying easy, portable games. Sushi Go was new. Each player had to try to build the best sushi meal. Trace waited until after I'd dug into my pancakes before pouncing.

She placed her next card. "Are you going to tell me what's going on?"

I smiled. "I whooped your butt with my wasabi card."

"Remi." Her tone implied I'd better come clean soon.

"Okay, okay." I laughed. I gathered up the cards and put them back in the tin. "Remember my stories of my Aunt's old manor house next to Alice's place?

She nodded. "One does not simply forget about a gothic castle in the middle of Virginia. It's why you chose this town for the event in the first place."

"I don't mean to eavesdrop, but are you talking about the old Kerr place?"

For the first time, I took a good look at our waiter. He was tall, dark-haired, wearing a shirt that outlined a well-toned, lean physique. I'm not sure how I missed him the first time. I blame shutting off my hormones after my breakup and the day's excitement. I nodded, taking a sip of my drink to give myself time to browse a bit more.

"You must be Remi." He laughed a nice, deep chuckle. "You look just like her." He pointed to a photo on the wall of a short, curvy brunette. "Chels, come out here. The new owner of Rosemary's place is here."

I cringed as Trace squealed. "Owner? Wait. Oh. My. God. She left the house to you? Her kids must be pis..." She turned to the table of kids next to us. "Furious." How long have you known, and how could you not have told me? Me?"

An older lady in jeans, a zebra print halter top, and bits of flour smudged on her face came out, loaded down with two plates piled high with pancakes. "Jake, honey, please don't yell." She set the plates at the table to our right before returning to us.

"Chels, this is Rosemary's niece," Jake said, motioning towards me. "She's moving into the old house."

I held up my hand, trying to decide which person to respond to first. I looked at Trace. "Um, surprise?"

"Does Mary know? She is going to have a cow and a half. Well, hon," Chelsea said. "Best of luck to you. I'm sure you've considered what you will do with the property. It would make a fantastic B&B or event location, and Don's Diner would be a perfect partner to help you pull in guests and market your brand." She said it all so fast it almost came out as one long word. I wondered how long she'd practiced that approach. I had stopped with a bite of pancake halfway to my mouth and looked over at Trace, who shrugged.

"I do have a plan, and that might be something we can talk about." I said.

"Rosemary would have appreciated it being used," Chelsea said. "She was never one to let the china waste away in the cupboard. Now, you'll need to try some of my homemade pecan pie. Jake, bring these ladies each a big slice."

If I didn't use her for food service, I could use her as my salesperson. She was like a bulldog. I held up both my hands in a feeble stop gesture. "This food is fantastic. I'm sure we can talk later. I haven't been inside the place since I was a kid." I handed Chelsea my card. "The work number is no good, but you can reach me on my cell."

"Just keep me in mind first. You're going to have people coming at you from all angles. I'm helping provide food up to Alice's this weekend, so you can see my work then."

I was surprised as we hadn't agreed to feed anyone during the event, but I'd check with Alice later.

"Most people are probably just wondering where Rosemary's husband is buried or where the jewels are hidden," Jake said, setting the slices in front of us.

This time I set my fork down. "Excuse me?"

Jake shook his head at the question and laughed. "This here's a small town. Rosemary was a loner who never quite fit in. There are stories that grew from stories."

Trace, who had been quiet throughout the whole exchange, suddenly smiled at me. "Best. Day. Ever."

Chapter Two

Jake brought over the bill and told us to take our time. The morning rush was starting to clear out, letting me see more of the retro diner decor from our corner table. Trying to read a sign on the far wall, I met the eyes of an imposing, red-haired man staring back at me. I smiled and immediately looked away. Out of the corner of my eye, I could tell he was still looking.

"Tell me everything," Trace said around a mouthful of pie.

"Right now, there's some lumberjack-looking dude staring rather rudely."

She didn't even bother to look. "No, about the house! And who is Mary? And taste that pie. It is pure heaven."

"Not a clue who Mary is." I shrugged. "Rosemary's lawyer Stan contacted me a month ago. It was the seventh anniversary since she went missing, so they declared her dead and officially read the will. I couldn't believe she left it for me. I haven't seen her since I was six, and I was only out here once before I started planning the event with Alice."

She reached over and squeezed my hand. "I'm sorry. It must still be weird in a way."

"A little." I looked down and took the final few bites of my pie. "She must have still been in contact with parts of the family. The will said she knew I could turn it into a successful game themed BnB." A dream of mine since high school.

"When do I get to see it?" Trace asked.

"As soon as I sign a few more papers. That's why we ended up coming early. Alice has the event setup completely in hand." It's not often I could surprise Trace, so I took a second to enjoy her reaction.

"So, we're not spending the next few days trekking through the woods hiding things?"

I was about to answer when I saw the red-haired man lumber up to our table.

"Sorry to interrupt, but I heard you mention hiking and wanted to offer my services."

He wore a welcoming smile, which complimented his ginger beard and hair. That was all overshadowed by the arrogance of pulling up a chair and sitting with us. Did no one in this town have boundaries? Cute freckles or not. He had to go.

"We're fine, thanks. And in the middle of something." Trace turned away from him, her whole focus on me.

"Hey lady, I'm trying to offer primo trekking guide time here." He reached toward her.

I reached for my glass of ice water at the same time, ready to douse him.

"Come on, Scott. Leave them alone. Here's your order." Jake stepped between him and Trace. He pushed a bag of food against his chest and waited until he got up and left. It might have been more fun to handle on our own, but it was probably best not to make a scene or an enemy on our first day.

Jake seemed to have him handled and out the door, so I went back to the happy news. "Anyway, let's wipe that from our day. The event is as ready as it can be. We need to check in with Alice to make sure she doesn't need anything. So, carb up, we have a house to explore."

Trace took out her phone and started typing. My stomach was full to bursting, but I eyed the last bite of pie on her plate.

"Okay, I let the cafe and the wildlife center know I would be gone a little longer than I thought, and they'd need to look for a replacement."

I sat there and looked at her, one eyebrow raised.

"Puh-lease. You expected me to believe that you were moving two hours away, but you weren't planning on asking me to partner up with you on running the place?"

I took a deep breath and pulled my purse into my lap.

"Wait. Are you?" She asked, a little softer.

Laughing, I showed her my phone with the website I'd mocked up with our names. Part of me was eager to jump up and go see the place. Part of me was scared of what I was going to find. An imposing, locked iron gate closed off the house, hiding it from the road. My 5'4 inch height wasn't enough for a peek-in over the fence. There was a vague path from Alice's place, but I hadn't gotten around to trying that yet. While Trace went to the restroom, I jotted down some notes on things I still needed to do.

Inheriting a house technically unseen and 'as is' left so much room for bad things. Expensive, bad things. I wanted life to be perfect and uncomplicated for a few more minutes. I now have my own home here in Northern Virginia. No more hearing the kids in the apartment next door or the upstairs neighbors vacuuming at two in the morning. I mean, seriously. Who does that? No job working me long hours for meaningless projects. No drama.

I looked up from my notes, thinking the person approaching was Chelsea.

"You. Cheater. Hustler!" A middle-aged woman in a soiled version of a Sunday's best dress stood about three feet away, pointing at my chest. "We all know you rigged something with the lawyer." She stepped close enough that I could smell a fermented liquid breakfast emanating from her. I turned my face away, my hand in front of my nose.

Jake stepped in, blocking her from getting any closer. That made two times in one morning. Someone has a knight in shining armor complex or he works as a bouncer part-time. His help was unnecessary, but it did feel nice to have a person other than Trace have my back. In time, he'd learn we could handle ourselves.

Her voice rose another octave. "I spent years helping her! That place should be mine! I was the reason they moved to declare her dead, and you just come traipsing in from the city and steal it away."

I focused on the tiny bit of spit on her lip; her cheeks puffed out in indignation. It all reminded me of a rabid squirrel. I slid out of the booth and stood, ready to head out. "You must be Mary." I didn't offer my hand. "I didn't rig anything. I was as surprised as anyone when I got the house."

Trace walked up to join our standoff, stifling a snort. "I can't leave you for two minutes, can I?"

"Mary, come on. I don't want to have to call the police on you again." Jake warned her.

"You should. Everyone needs to know what she's done. I will never let you have that house." She turned and stomped out through the front door.

"Well, she's not going to throw you a welcome to the neighborhood party." Trace said. "What the fudge was all that?"

"I'll take 'What is a potential sore loser for two hundred, Alex," I said, signing the credit card bill. I shook my head, trying to clear it of the craziness from the last few minutes. Jake and Chelsea waved bye as I grabbed a mint from the counter on our way out. At the door, I scanned the parking lot for my new arch nemesis and glanced over my car for any keying marks or slit tires.

"I'll drive a bit," Trace offered.

I handed over the keys. The confrontations had unsettled me. In one morning, I've had two run-ins and a body bag. "We need to pop into town quickly so I can make this all official." I took a few slow, deep breaths. Welcome or not. I was here to stay.

The town's main street was only a few blocks away and suited the diner. I loved taking time to walk around the shops on my previous trips to do weekend prep work. Quaint but clean. Franchises were scattered throughout, but several mom-and-pop shops guaranteed some local flavor. They would provide any shopping I needed. I hoped to partner with some of the shops when my business opened. I chuckled, knowing that Chelsea would be on board.

Trace left to wander the town while I dealt with the legal paperwork. It was not entirely signed in blood, but I needed to sign a few forms to get a key. The property had not been maintained outside of some basics. If I fell through the floor to my death, the lawyer Stan Fletcher, advised me that wouldn't be the legal firm's problem. Stan was a portly man in his late fifties. He gave the impression that if an alien ship landed directly in front of him, he might rouse himself to proclaim it 'interesting.'

"I need to inform you that there have been several offers on the home since we last spoke," Stan said.

"I'm not interested."

"Understood. However, I do need to present them to you. Two are significantly more than market value. We can discuss them when you are ready."

I nodded and took the sealed packet from him. "Thanks, but I'm set on turning it into a BnB as soon as possible."

He looked at the envelope. "Yes, In there I've also provided you an itemized breakdown of your requirements to make that possible. Rosemary had advised me that would be your plan. There will be permits to obtain, of course. However, as no one opposes your business they should be a formality."

Unease tickled my spine remembering Mary, but what could I do? I thanked Stan for his efforts, clutched my paperwork to me, and went to find Trace. The business advice he provided was priceless. More importantly, for our immediate needs, he provided a hand-drawn map. Even though my land butted up to Alice's farm, the entrance was off a private road I hadn't seen in over twenty years. Stan assured me we wouldn't miss it. I felt I could prove him wrong.

I met up with Trace, and in a few minutes of driving, we turned off the main road onto an unpaved track. Partially hidden behind some overgrowth was a tall, gothic iron gate. I took a selfie with the key before unlocking and pushing against the gates. It took both of us to move them enough for a car to go in. Those would need some work, or I would need to take up weightlifting to get them open and closed.

"Do you want me to stop ahead so you can try to close them?" Trace asked.

I shook my head as I settled back into my seat, sweating from the effort. The driveway was a pitted dirt road lined with old trees on both sides, providing an escort down the lane. I caught glimpses of the stone turret through the thick trees and excitedly tapped my toes. What girl doesn't dream of growing up and living in a castle? Okay, stop it, Remi. Stay grounded until you know what you're facing.

I pointed to the structure appearing through the leaves. "We made it."

At the end of the foliage, Trace stopped the car. If Wednesday Addams married someone from Braveheart and then abandoned the home to the elements, you'd just about have the Kerr residence. I couldn't love it more. The driveway led up to the front door of the three-story stone mansion. At one time the driveway must have been covered in decorative pebbles, but now only a few stray stones remained amongst the dirt. In the center of the circular driveway was a dried-up fountain; the statue of a lady archer and a deer, tilted, ready to topple over in its center.

The car had barely stopped when I opened the door and stepped out. I mentally rolled up my sleeves. The large wrap-around porch was cluttered with chairs that didn't look safe, and the bushes in front of it needed an emergency appointment with a hedge trimmer. Beyond the chairs and overgrowth, an oversized front door beckoned me forward. I avoided the middle of the stairs as I walked up to the porch, unsure if there was wood rot to deal with.

I looked over at Trace, wanting to see her impression, but frowned as she gazed into the distance. "You're looking the wrong way, and this is where you're supposed to ooh and aah."

She turned back to look at me. "I'm ooh'ing on the inside, But I'm also wondering who the heck that is."

Trace pointed to the field beyond the house, where I could see the top of a large, domed, blue tent. The grass between us was knee-high and didn't offer a clear path from the house to the tent.

"Huh, well from the map, this backs to a park, so it might just be a camper who wandered to the wrong area." I was too jacked up about getting into the house to worry about it.

I jiggled the key a bit to get the lock moving. The Virginia humidity had swollen the arched door firmly shut. Lacking WD40, my muscles got tested again, even with the key. The door protested at being put back to work. We managed to push it enough to squeeze in. It's a good thing we didn't eat a second serving of pancakes. I pulled a leather-bound notebook and a pen from my bag and jotted the first of many notes. 'Door adjustment needed.'

I slid my hand along the wall and flipped the switch. Fingers crossed that the orders to turn on all the utilities had gone through. "And there was light!" A sad flicker in the ceiling came from the sole working lightbulb in the chandelier.

Flipping upon the notebook again, I added, 'Buy lightbulbs.'

"You're going to need a bigger notebook," Trace teased.

I learned one of Rosemary's secrets from the feeble light coming from the one working bulb. She had been a bit of a hoarder. The entryway was filled floor to ceiling with boxes and stuffed trash bags. No wonder they can't find her husband.

Trace squeezed in beside me. "Wow. Maybe her husband just got lost in all this somewhere. It might be easier to bushwhack to that tent and see if we can crash there for the night."

"We're staying at Alice's." I pointed down the box-filled hallway. "The small path to the kitchen is all we can do right now anyway. The inspection found termite damage, and they're tenting the house tomorrow."

"Eww...bugs." She looked around as if a giant B movie-sized termite was lying in the shadows.

"No worries. Tenting will clean it up, and the lawyers have repairs scheduled. Staying on this one path is just a safety precaution."

I picked up a plastic flamingo lying on the box beside me and solemnly held it before me. "This, and all you see before us, is ours."

She placed her hand on the flamingo's head. "I accept the sacred flamingo of home ownership. But we're going to need reinforcements," Trace said as she scooted past the boxes lining the hallway. She turned in and grinned at me. "How about we ask that cute waiter guy if he wants to earn money helping us clean up?"

I could feel the blush creeping up my cheeks, having a few thoughts about Jake. "He's too young. Besides, I've sworn off men. Or relationships. I want to focus on moving my dreams forward." I put my hand on the ornate chair railing, smiling.

"No, you've sworn off worthless men who don't deserve you." She turned and started walking off down the hall. "And honestly, we'll need some local help to haul all this out so we can see what we have to work with. After we scrounge for treasures, of course."

"Valid point." Despite the overwhelming work ahead, I giggled as I followed her down the hall. "Can you believe this place??"

She laughed, seeing me still clutching the flamingo. "Best. Day. Ev..." The word 'ever' died as we walked into the kitchen.

Chapter Three

We stopped in the doorway of a commercial-grade stainless steel kitchen. It would have been a chef's dream if not for the shattered glass from the door and broken dishes.

"What the..." Trace said from behind me.

I bent down and picked up a rock. It was a hot, windless summer day, so no freak windstorm had blown it through the window or caused the dishes to smash on the floor. The smell of paint hit seconds before I noticed the words GIT OUT scrawled across the wall in bright red.

"Seriously?" I laid the rock on the kitchen island. "Great. Vandals who don't even have the common decency to spell properly." I stopped and took a deep, calming breath. "I guess I should call the police. It's not too late to text the cafe back and say you want to stay."

"Are you nuts? They don't know who they're messing with." She fist-bumped me.

The back door had been left ajar. I guess my unpleasant guests were hoping animals would come in and do more damage. I walked over to close it.

"Ma'am."

I yelped and stepped back as a man appeared in the opening. I think it was only his police uniform that saved him from Trace swinging a broom at his head.

He raised his hands and stepped backward. "Sorry to startle you. I'm Sheriff Marrow." He nodded at Trace. "Ms. Cooper." His white crew-cut length hair and beard emphasized his no-nonsense expression but clashed with the ketchup stain on his pocket. This man would not appreciate any shenanigans. I couldn't help myself.

"That's some mighty quick response time for a non-emergency call that I haven't even made yet," I said.

"I beg your pardon?" he asked, his brow furrowed.

I opened the door and gestured to the graffitied wall. "My welcome to the neighborhood gift. I would have preferred a taco dip."

"Oh, huh..." he scratched his head. "I am sorry to see that, ma'am. Do you want to file a report?"

"I probably should for insurance's sake, if nothing else," I said, stepping aside to let him in.

"Let me take a few photos and get started." He pulled out his phone and a notepad. "Has anyone given you any trouble that you can think of?"

"Crazy diner lady," Trace said and explained our morning adventure. She busied herself sweeping up broken crockery.

"Mary." He shook his head. "She can be a bit of a handful at times. If she's drinking again, I could see her doing something like this. She would have a key, though, and wouldn't need to break in."

I mentally added 'change all locks' to my list.

"What's her problem with me?" I asked.

He talked while he worked. "Mary was Rosemary's live-in housekeeper for years. She probably assumed Rosemary would leave her the place."

Housekeeper? I looked back at the towering boxes that lined the hallway. I don't think I'd hire her.

"Look, I don't think I'll press charges if it was her. Let's hope this is the end of it. Maybe I can get her to be okay with this. If there's nothing else, I need to get this door covered up with some cardboard." I stopped for a moment. "I didn't hear a car pull up. Where did you park? Why are you even here?"

"Well ma'am, there's a pull-off near the creek that people use for fishing and hiking." He gestured with the pad of paper in his hands to the right of the house where the tent was. Maybe a ten-minute walk from here."

"That combined with no one coming through that front gate anytime recently does confirm the graffiti had to be someone local. No one else would know about that," I said.

"A Doug would," Trace added.

"True," I agreed.

"Who is Doug?" He clicked his pen, poised to write.

I waved it away. "There's nothing to jot down. Doug is an old friend who would Google Satellite Map everywhere he went. He could tell you the color of your parent's house from three states away and if their flowers were blooming. Doug would have known how to get here from the creek."

"Where is Doug now?"

I pulled up my phone. "His last check-in was fifteen minutes ago at Starbucks in Los Angeles. Not Doug."

"People should be more careful about always letting people know where they are." He shook his head as he handed me his business card. "You might think about getting some outside motion lights."

"Thanks. I will put them on my ever-growing list of things to buy. Aren't you going to check for fingerprints or anything for the report?" I asked.

"You handled the rock, and I don't see any footprints on the ground, or anything dropped on my way over here." He looked towards the tent. "Are you aware someone is camping on your land?"

"We saw it but didn't wade through the grass to see what they were doing. Do you think it's a problem?" I asked.

"I'll check there again on my way out. Someone probably didn't realize they'd wandered onto private land. I left them a note with my information. In the meantime, make sure you're locked in tonight." He nodded to Trace before heading back out the door towards the woods.

I kind of hoped it was Mary. I didn't need more than one person trying to get me out of town. I knew the sheriff wouldn't be able to do much other than file a report and get this on record. At least his odd sudden appearance saved me a phone call. Even in a small town, there was bound to be a more urgent crime to investigate. I pulled out my phone and texted Stan with pictures and updates while Trace assembled supplies to clean the wall. Acetone in nail polish remover is fantastic for cleaning ink off rubber stamps and handy for paint on walls. It wouldn't fix it, but at least a fresh layer of paint won't have stark red to try to cover. I wasn't a huge fan of the butter yellow throughout the kitchen anyway.

It didn't take long before sweat dripped down my back. Fixing the air conditioning moved to spot number one on my list. We had the letters down to a faded look and decided to stop for drinks.

"How about we chill on the front porch? At least than we could hope for a cool breeze." Trace suggested. She threw me the pack of travel wipes she'd used to clean her face and arms. "I'll grab some snacks too."

Planters dotted the wraparound porch. They were full of sticks and dried leaves that were once living plants. A couple of rocking chairs looked like they had held up. I sat gingerly in one, testing the stability.

"So, is this when you're going to tell me how the nice sheriff knew your name and happened to be in the area?" I asked.

She stopped mid-chew of a carrot, her eyes going wide. I watched as she chewed and moved the other carrots around on her paper plate. I leaned back and propped my feet on the railing. I had all day.

"I, uh, checked in when I got to town." She toyed with a carrot stick. "You know, while you were getting the papers taken care of. He said he'd be sure to keep an eye out. I guess he was doing a courtesy check of the place."

I waited while she picked up the same carrot stick three times. There was more to this story.

"So, the weird phone calls I was getting might have turned into more", she said quietly.

"More? Like what more exactly?" I swung my feet down and leaned over to her.

She opened her texts to show me a picture of her in the diner this morning. The text read, 'I can't wait to spend the weekend with you.'

"How is that possible?" I clenched my teeth, trying to calm myself. I was willing to believe the calls were just mistakes, but this was too far. "Did you text back?"

She frowned. "It doesn't accept incoming messages."

I racked my brain trying to visualize everyone we saw this morning, but it was a sea of faces. "Did anyone in the diner look familiar?" I asked.

"No. I don't even want to think about this right now. The police know. I can't do anything except work myself up, and I'd rather put all that energy into helping you this weekend. Besides, if we're moving boxes, I will build up my triceps. If the jerk ever approaches me, I can knock him on his...."

I put a hand on her shoulder and motioned at a man walking towards us from the direction of the tent.

"Hello!" he yelled out.

Not a fan of unexpected visitors and on edge from stalker talk, I stood up and moved in front of Trace. A piece of wood and another plastic flamingo were within reach to use as weapons.

He looked mid-twenties, wearing one of those fisherman vests with all the pockets, canvas shorts with more pockets, and what looked like a safari hat. The hat he removed on his walk towards us. He was a cartoon of an adventurer as his clothing lacked to reality of dirt smudging the ironed lines.

Once he reached us, he offered a handshake. I crossed my arms. Murder podcast rule number one: It was better to be rude than dead.

He put his hand back down, his smile never dimming. "Sorry to barge in like this. I'm Nathan. It seems I'm camping in your backyard. Just thought I'd come by and introduce myself."

"We were thinking of going out to see you earlier but couldn't figure out a good path." I moved aside so he could see that I wasn't alone.

"Ah, yeah, you have to go into the trees a bit over there to meet up with the park trail." He took off his hat and ran his fingers through his curly blond hair.

"Look, I'm sorry about being on your land and all. I was walking the main trail to the Appalachian and needed to take a break. This was the first clearing I came across. The house looked abandoned, so I figured no one would care."

"How long have you been there?" Trace asked. Her crossed arms mimicked mine.

"Just today." He rested a foot on the bottom stair, the aged wood bent in as if threatening to break. He was poised and relaxed, his hands in his pockets.

"Did you happen to see anyone come up here earlier?" I asked.

"Nah, I was in town until now, restocking. Why?" He asked, his smile starting to seem as fake as the rest of him.

"Looks like someone broke in. If you see or hear anything, please contact the police. I believe they left you a card." I hope my implied threat of the cops knowing about him would be a deterrent. "We need to get going." I looked over towards his tent. "Sorry to rush you along, but we have people coming to work on the house and yard. You'll need to move your camp today."

He nodded, but I wasn't sure it was in response to moving his tent. "Hey, you two moving in here? You ladies might need someone around the house to, ya know, do handyman stuff. I'm your guy." He smiled and leaned around me to speak to Trace. "I could arrange to stick around a bit."

"We're good, thanks," Trace said. "Good luck on the trail." She pointed towards his tent as a clear dismissal.

I took the opportunity to snap a photo of him.

His eyes lingered on Trace for another moment before putting his hat back on and walking away.

"Let's wait a sec to make sure he goes back to his tent." I said.

Trace packed the last of our picnic supplies up. "Something creepy about that guy," she said

Chapter Four

I laid my hand on the front door as we locked up. "See ya soon, old girl." This weekend was about our event, and it was time to go help. If it weren't for the scheduled pesticide tenting, I would throw a sleeping bag down on the dirty floor and camp here. All those years of binging DIY shows will finally pay off.

"Will the taped-up cardboard be enough protection for the kitchen?" Trace asked.

I shrugged. I had half a day of homeowner knowledge. "It'll hopefully keep the animals out. Or at least any animals that hadn't already made a home here. I'll schedule the repair as soon as it's safe to go back in."

"Why don't we just keep the car parked here and take that path you mentioned to Alice's?"

I motioned to the file boxes still squishing her overnight bag in the backseat. "Do you want to lug all that stuff?"

"Fair point. Let's drive next door." She said, hopping back into the driver's seat. "I can't wait to meet them in person."

"They are amazing." I leaned back into the seat. "I can't believe my life right now. It was only a few months ago I met Alice at the rubber stamp carving class and started planning this event. Now I'll be living beside her. It just seems too unreal."

"You rolled a natural twenty, my friend. Next stop, Alice and Jason's place."

"Looks like things started early," Trace said as we pulled up to a white Victorian farmhouse. Several people milled about, and tents dotted the large field to the left of Alice's front door. The event didn't begin until tomorrow, and most folks weren't due until Saturday. What the heck was going on?

"Alrighty, Remi. It looks like we need to jump right in, so walk me through this." Trace reached behind me for one of the folders I'd packed. She was new to my favorite hobby of letterboxing, but jumping in to volunteer was something she loved to do. Besides, both our jobs had kept us so busy of late that we were overdo for some best-friend time.

"Okay. Quick and dirty recap. Letterboxing is essentially hiding a carved rubber stamp with a blank book in a Tupperware-type box and then leaving clues for people to find it. These are clues to boxes already in the area."

She quickly flipped through the printed pages and pointed at the rubber duck image on the cover.

"That's me," I said. "People tend to take on a letterboxing name. Mine is Rubber Duckie, so I carved a stamp resembling a rubber duck to represent me. When I find the hidden box, I ink the stamp and place my duck image in their logbook. Then I take the themed stamp they've left in the box and stamp it in my book. Got it?"

"Follow clues. Find a box. Let's start with that. Also, I love that you're Rubber Ducky."

Trace had bought me my first themed rubber duck as a souvenir from a trip to Iceland. Now, I had a whole box of ducks. Each one memorializes a different adventure. Ducks were also the base inspiration for the theme of this weekend's event - Invasion of the Rubber Duckies,

Not seeing Alice or her husband Jason, I placed some Martian-themed toy rubber ducks on a table she'd set up on the porch. Then, I propped up a corkboard, added a bunch of extra pins in the top corner, and started the word-of-mouth clues by pinning one onto the board. It said, "Even evil alien ducks love water. Find the best source of water in town and think like a duck. You'll find your duck right up against the wall. Warning: Don't wear long sleeves." Word-of-mouth clues were ones never posted online.

"Remi!" Alice pushed the door with her foot while wrapping her long, greying hair into a low, messy bun. She gave me a welcoming hug. "I was starting to worry you got lost."

Trace wisely stayed silent.

"Trace! It's so good to finally have you here." Alice enveloped her in a hug as well.

"Sorry, Alice, we ended up stopping at the diner and picking up the keys to the house," I said.

"Did you try the strawberry pie? If I keep eating that, I'll need to start getting more exercise." She laughed as she patted her stomach. Slightly plump but still fit from the manual labor around her farm, I didn't think she could become more active. She put most of my younger friends to shame with how much she got done in a single day. She laced her arm through mine and stopped. "House? What house?"

"We're going to be neighbors!" I laughed and explained.

"You've got to tell Jason. He's been dying to see the inside of that old place."

We followed her into the front foyer. "Hopefully, you can both give me some tips. It's going to take some work to get it fixed up." I admired the dark wood flooring they had only finished up last month.

Alice and Jason had bought this old place a few years ago with the plan to fix it up over time and retire here. After Jason had a health scare on his fortieth birthday, they decided life was too short to wait on their dream. Now, they work to simplify their lives and cut costs. Things like solar panels, growing their food, and up-cycling what they could. Alice created beautiful scenic quilts from scraps and made mosaic art from cut-up soda cans to sell at the local craft fairs.

"Well, of course we will!" She grabbed a small sketchbook from the front table. "But right now, I have a box to track down."

"I thought you helped hide all the boxes?" Trace asked.

"Seems a few people snuck some on the trails last weekend, and I figure this is the last chance I'll get before more people arrive."

"Alone?" Trace asked.

Alice shrugged. "Jason is trying to finish getting the downstairs bathroom prepped for paint. I'll be glad to see the last of that awful paisley wallpaper." She addressed me with that last part. "But the rooms are ready, and I hope you enjoy the extra touches. This rubber duck theme was so much fun to play with."

"Extras?" I asked. "I'm intrigued."

"You'll just have to be surprised." She grinned, looking pleased with herself.

"I can't wait. I need to plant one more set of ducks today. I can't believe the turnout."

"If you have a bit of time first, can you help anyone else that shows up? Word got out about this around town, and a bunch of locals decided to come play. We're letting people camp here. All the hotels in the area are booked solid with the annual UFO weekend."

"I wondered what was up with the people outside," I said. "Why do the locals need a place to stay?"

Alice laughed. "They are taking advantage of the need and renting their places out."

I nodded. "Not a problem. I've got things here." I gestured around. "I can't wait to see what this festival is like."

Trace bit her lower lip. A sure sign she was concerned. I knew Alice spent much of her time walking the trails alone and would probably end up teaching Trace a thing or two about trail safety. Still, all Trace saw was a lone woman heading out alone.

"Trace, you did say you wanted to try letterboxing. You'll probably enjoy it more with someone else who's also new to it. You know how bad I am at keeping secrets!"

Alice clapped her hands. "Wonderful! I've heard so much about you, Trace, that I'd love the chance to chat. It's always good to have company."

I pulled open my personal clue folder and gave them a copy of the clues for Drunken Wanderer. "In case you love the first one and want another to do. I did this one last time I was up. It's a beautiful walk with some fairly straightforward clues. Do you both have a stamp?"

Trace had the one I had carved for her of a cat curled around a coffee mug. She would use the name Coffee Cat as her letterboxing trail name.

"I started one after our carving class. It's not quite done, though."

If that was what Alice considered not entirely done, she was a natural at carving. It was a beautiful image mimicking the basic outline of their house with details put in to add windows and the large, rounded door. "You've got the knack for it. Is there any craft you can't conquer?" I asked, impressed.

She blushed at the compliment.

Trace grabbed her stamp, blank book, and a handful of assorted ink pads and put them in a small messenger bag she wore across her chest.

"You won't need a compass for mine. Just be sure to re-hide it well," I said.

"And I have extra water packed if we need it. Ready?" Alice asked.

They turned to leave just as a couple in their late twenties hurried up to us, books clutched in their hands.

"Wait! Are you Rubber Duckie? Are you giving out event clues now?" They looked at the pages Trace held in her hand.

"I'm Movie Buff or Russ. This is Safari Sue," he announced.

Looking at them, I never would have paired them with those names. Sue's ironed pink polo shirt and khaki shorts matched her salon-tipped nails. Russ had a mop of curly red hair and freckles. He reminded me of shows where a fugitive shops for clothes at the gas station.

"We weren't going to bother you, but we saw you with a folder." Russ did the talking while Sue hung back a bit. I watched her grab a hair tie from her pocket and put her long blond hair back in a ponytail.

"Yes, I'm Rubber Duckie or Remi." I shooed Trace and Alice off, letting them know I could handle things. "No event clues until tomorrow. That was just something to help my friend practice. BUT there are plenty of local boxes you could search for today. I have copies printed out."

Sue ignored the clues I tried to hand her. She put on her sunglasses, her attention focused on Alice and Trace. "You know this is my first time trying this too. I'll catch up to them and see if I can tag along."

"Oh, um..." I pulled out my phone. "Just a sec," I said to Russ, sending Trace a quick text telling her to ping me if she didn't want the extra company.

Russ shrugged. "I already printed the local ones but don't remember anything starting in that direction. He pulled out a sheaf of papers from a travel-worn backpack.

"Looks like you started already," I said, looking at his hands smudged with different ink colors.

He smiled. "I stopped at the park before trying out the diner. Sue and I were sitting at the counter while you were there." He looked down at his hands. "You, uh, certainly made an impression on the town." He said, grimacing a little.

Not wanting to get into my personal life with someone I just met, I ignored the opening to explain what the ruckus at the diner was about. I motioned towards the three walking away. "They're doing a word-of-mouth one. No worries, though. The clue will be posted on the table tomorrow. There is one on the board now."

I walked with him over to the porch. He scribbled down the short clue provided.

"Are you camping?" I asked.

"No, Alice is letting a few of us stay in her barn. We had booked at the hotel in town, but thanks to some UFO sightings, rooms were given to the highest bidder. All prior reservations at the regular rates were conveniently lost, and the new rates they quoted were crazy. The other motels were even worse.

"A UFO sighting? Crazy. We planned the alien duck theme to match with the UFO festival this weekend, but that's the first I've heard of a sighting. I'm sorry about that." Alice had said that the festival was small and quirky. She has undersold it. Hopefully, this new wrinkle wouldn't cause trouble.

"It worked out," he shrugged.

"Let me know if there is anything I can do for you all. We'll give out packets tomorrow, but I'm happy to give out the lists of places to eat and tourist areas nearby tonight." Alice had prepped me with all of that over the week. "Come to think of it, I'll leave them on the table." I pulled out a few more sheets of paper and used a rock to make sure stray wind didn't blow them away. Even though the day had started muggy, Virginia weather meant we could have a variety of weather in a day. It was best to be prepared.

UFOs and hotels throwing people out did not bode well for a carefree event. Worried that Alice would have issues finding space for everyone, I said my goodbyes to get inside and check with Jason on the rooming issue. I hoped the event wouldn't be a disaster before it even began. This event will be a trial run for future events I'd want to hold and I wanted the guests happy.

I used my phone to pull up the event page and sent a quick note to all - 'please check on your reservations. If you find any issues, let us know, as we might have a solution if you don't mind camping or sharing a room.'

Trace and I could double up and leave a room free if the worst came to worst. Remembering the weird photo on her phone, I was tempted to do that anyway.

Chapter Five

I ran into Jason in the foyer. Literally, "Oops, sorry," I said.

He laughed and enveloped me into a bear hug before picking up the scraper he'd dropped. My head only came to chest level on his 6'2 frame. His hair was shaggy and mussed as if he'd been crawling around dusty areas, which he probably had. I looked around the foyer this time, marveling at how it had changed from my first visit. The drab gray entryway with peeling wallpaper had been turned into a welcoming area of maple wainscoting, a tasteful table with a signing book, and a jewel-colored area rug. A large painting of an old farmhouse with a lady shooing crows away took up most of the hallway wall.

"What's the rush, Remi?"

The only thing he loved even close to how much he loved Alice was this house and all the renovations he'd been making. Except for a few things he'd needed to call in extra hands for, he and Alice made every change through long back-breaking nights.

"If you've suddenly dug a pool I can cool off in, I'm first in line, but I doubt I'd be so lucky," I said. "Mainly, I was looking for you to see how many people you have staying here now." I gestured out the window to the tents.

"Hard to say. You and Trace have the top floor main rooms, but the other rooms have all become sort of a hiking hostel with people asking if they can share and throwing a sleeping bag on the floor. I think one person might be sleeping in a cast iron tub." He shrugged as if to say, 'To each his own.'

"I am so sorry, Jason. This is not at all what should have happened."

He laughed, shaking his head. "Oh, don't worry. Alice's nobody's fool. She's getting a fair rate for the rooms while still being accommodating, and now everyone can stay here together instead of all over town. The ones that have called seem to prefer this kind of casual bunking. We did have to tell them that breakfast wasn't included with the cost of the room, I mean T-shirt."

I remembered that little loophole. This place couldn't operate as a paying inn yet, but they could sell T-shirts and let people spend the night.

He continued. "Except for our original guests, who bought the deluxe cotton T-shirts. They will get breakfast. And to be honest, the bit of extra money coming in from the tent spaces will be useful in getting us finished on time." He nodded as he spoke as if mentally adding up final costs. "Oh, and we have about six people camping off to the side of the herb garden."

He seemed unperturbed by the additions to the weekend, and his ease rubbed off on me. I had to learn to let go of things I had no control over.

"I don't think we're due to have anyone else show up today. I know Alice is off, but I'll be in the downstairs basement scraping off more wallpaper if you need me. You're the first one of the house guests to arrive. Well, you and Trace." He grabbed a rag from his pocket and wiped some sweat from his face. "The air conditioning is out downstairs and it's like a sauna. Where is Trace? I've been looking forward to meeting her."

"She went off into the woods with Alice."

"Okay. I'm sure I'll hear all about that later. Here, let me give you Trace's key, too. No one else on your floor is due until this evening so it should be quiet. Relax. Enjoy yourself a bit."

He stopped a few steps down the hallway and turned back to me. "Oh. Let me help get your bags to your room." He started to put his tools down. Jason occasionally forgot about innkeeper duties, leaving that up to Alice. The handyman aspects of working the inn were his part.

"Don't worry about it." I picked up my bag. "I know you're dying to get back to things." I looked up the wooden stairs. "I love the colors you used. I'm in the purple room on the right?" I was referring to the largest room on the third and highest floor. He nodded.

I started up the stairs, waving Jason onto his work. Thank heavens Alice was the people-oriented one. Jason wouldn't last a day alone with a house full of guests. They'd feel like part of the family, but he'd probably forget to feed them. I almost called him back to tell him about my house, but it could wait. I walked up the stairs to a hallway with three doors and made my way to mine. Trace would be in the one named Isolde across the hall. Mine was officially named Camelot according to the door. Still, I had dubbed it the bunny room, so called by me due to a giant bunny painting hanging on one wall. Now, it was an adorable bunny in a garden, but it didn't scream Camelot to me. The other room was taken by a couple coming for their first letterboxing event. As of now, it could be taken by far more than that, but I refused to let that bother me. I would adopt Jason's carefree attitude and take a few minutes to marvel at how much life had changed. Right after I finished prep work and made a list of things to do.

I opened the door and stopped to peer at the back to see that it did indeed say Camelot. The room didn't look the same as when I was last here. The only things still here I remembered were the royal purple bedding and various embroidered pillows. There were minimal knickknacks before, as Alice wasn't big on items without a purpose, but now there were ducks. I mean, a lot of ducks. Rubber ducks and spaceships. Even my large bunny painting over the dresser was now a painting of a small coastal town with UFOs beaming down into the buildings and small shapes caught rising in the beams. It was overdone and kitschy, and I loved it more than I could say.

The door to my ensuite was open, and I mentally thanked Jason and Alice for the new soaking tub along the back wall. I threw my overnight bag into the room, not one to unpack when only staying somewhere for a brief time. In here the temperature was comfortable. There was a long, soothing bubble bath in my future, and I was thrilled I wasn't sharing a room or bathroom with anyone else. But willpower had to override desire. I wondered if they had done this to everyone's rooms or just mine?

With everything else calling my attention, I almost missed the tented sign on my bed: "Welcome to the Rubber Duck Invasion. Your innkeepers, Alice and Jason, have designed your room to maximize your weekend. Alice is a huge puzzle geek and has hidden clues and red herrings to the location of the Golden Duck. The first to figure it out gets a free weekend when we officially open. Runners-up get treats as well."

It was official. I wanted them to adopt me. I couldn't believe they had done all this on top of their other work. Golden Duck, eh? I walked to the dresser to look closer at my ducks, wondering how they were clues. I turned them over and saw a word written under one of them: "Birds." I examined each of the ducks in turn to see if I missed anything more. If that was all I had to start with, I was stumped. I was pleased she wasn't going to make this easy.

I scrounged through my backpack and opened a spare notebook to the back to record the word and my room name in case it mattered. I wrote down how many ducks were in my room and took a photo of them and the UFO painting with my phone. From the window, I could see a turret peeking through the treetops and I stopped to stare. It was mine, mine, mine. I resisted the urge to open my notebook and jot down notes of what I wanted to do and what games I should have on hand. My phone hadn't brought me any news from the police on the vandalism. To be fair, chances were low that it would come to anything.

I shoved the house to the back of my mind and headed outside. I stopped on the porch to check in with Trace while I had cell service. Her response did not thrill me.

Chapter Six

"Ran into Scott, the guy from the diner, who wanted to see what letterboxing was. Then, two other letterboxers joined in. All good. We'll talk later." Trace included a selfie of the six of them on the trail.

At least she was with a group. I planned to plant four duck stamps on the two-mile loop walk around the farmhouse. All carvings of different rubber duck aliens with only one logbook at the end of the series, so people didn't have to stop and stamp their own image each time.

Once outside, I did a final check of my supplies. I put each stamp in a pre-made felt envelope-style bag and then into a small Tupperware container. The last box would also house the logbook. It's sort of a guestbook where they could log in that they found the stamps.

"Last minute prep?" A dark-haired man said in a low, gravelly voice. He smiled and held out his hand. "Nick, um, Green Archer.

You must be Rubber Ducky." He nodded at my T-shirt that read Release the Quacken over a Godzilla-sized rubber duck terrorizing a city.

He was cute in a geeky way I appreciated. Kind of floppy, dark hair, glasses, tall and lanky, with high cheekbones. He wore a T-shirt stating 'All Who Wander Are Not Lost.'

"You caught me duck-handed. I only finished carving these yesterday, so I need to plant them."

He secured his backpack straps more firmly in place and pulled out two well-used trekking poles. "Mind if I go along? This is my first event, and honestly, I haven't even done any letterboxing yet." He shrugged, seemingly embarrassed by the admission. "I heard about it from my hiking club and thought it would be a great camping weekend."

I looked around and realized it was just Nick and I outside. Everyone else must've been out hiking. My urban brain yelled at me, 'No, you will not go off into the woods with a man you met three seconds ago.' The other side of my brain screamed, 'Take Trace's advice and just have fun. His voice is like listening to a cat purr. Go, go, go.' I decided to merge them and be a good yet safety-conscious co-host. I did remember seeing his name on the sign-up list.

"Sure, let me just tell Jason and text my friend Trace so she knows where we're going and when to expect us back." I felt I sounded paranoid as soon as I said it. "You know, in case anyone else shows up and is looking for us, um, me. For the event and all." While pretending to type, I snapped a quick photo of him to send with my text to Trace. Maybe I should stop listening to so many murder podcasts.

After I received a thumbs-up emoji confirmation from Trace that all was also okay with her, I waved him ahead to lead the way. "Hey, how about you follow the clues to where they'll be placed? It'll allow me to test them and make sure they make sense."

Nick shrugged and took the clue from me. "Follow some directions. Not a problem. We're off to find the Martial Duck."

The clues for this were step-by-step, in case someone wanted to try it at night or for a quick find without going too far away. Alice and I had worked to pepper the event with various easy-to-hard clues, and the same with the hikes. If you wanted to get them all, there were some challenging uphill hikes and some mysteries to solve. But if you just wanted leisurely strolls and straightforward answers, you could still come away with some beautifully carved images and hopefully a great time.

Nick read it aloud to himself, but I knew where to head: *"You hear a strange sound, so you decide to go investigate. You obviously haven't seen enough horror movies and know that is never a good idea, but you go anyway. Starting from the house, take the walking trail at the end of the driveway. Pass a bench and take the first trail on the left. You occasionally see flashes of yellow light illuminating the sky. What could be going on? I'm sure it's nothing. Walk, don't run, until you see three fallen logs over the path."*

He started to read the next paragraph, but I stopped him. "No need to read the whole clue right now. We have enough to get us started." I snapped my backpack on and set off on the trail.

The sweat dripping down my back reminded me why Fall was my favorite season. Part of me wished I was alone, but hiking with a buddy was safer. And to be honest, there was no guarantee I wouldn't get lost, even on a loop trail. I may have loved letterboxing, but I wasn't a nature girl. I wouldn't shriek if a spider appeared next to me, but my outside experience was usually with a book and a porch swing. My hiking shoes were only slightly more worn than Trace's.

Nick didn't seem inclined to break the silence of our walk, and I appreciated being spared small talk, especially about careers. Living so close to Washington, D.C., jobs were a hot topic. I rarely cared what someone did for a living unless it was unusual. I've never felt that just knowing what a person did to pay their bills gave a true insight into who they were. My own dead-end job as an auditor was in my past and the last thing I wanted to talk about.

Lost in my daydreaming, I was startled when Nick cleared his throat and tilted his head to the right. I looked over and saw a bench half-hidden by overgrowth and was about to give him a look of "So?" when I remembered I wasn't out on a random walk. The bench. "Right, so here's our trail up ahead. Next, we're looking for the three fallen trees, and then we'll need the compass to go to a heading of 150 degrees."

We didn't have far to go until we found them. I saw Nick pull out his compass and debated if I should tell him he had the thing turned the wrong way around. Keep it flat to line up the arrow with North. Then follow where 150 degrees is. "Clue says that we were to take 20 paces into the woods and search behind the tree under some rocks."

He started to take regular steps as he counted.

"It said paces."

"Is that some strange clue?"

"In a clue, paces are the equivalent of two steps," I said.

He put his foot forward as if we were playing a game of Simon Sez and was told to take a giant step forward.

I couldn't help it and giggled. "Just a regular step, but two of them," I said. I held my tongue the rest of the time while Nick found the box with only a few false starts.

"Once you find the area, it does sort of jump out at you as being slightly out of place," he mentioned as he moved a suspicious pile of rocks to the side, revealing a small Tupperware box. He had a contagious smile that lit up like it was Christmas morning as he pulled the box out. He popped the lid off and looked at me with his eyebrow raised as the only thing in the box was a small piece of lined paper that read: "Martial Duck."

I held the stamp up for him. "Remember, we're here so I can plant the series? When I did the first walkthrough, I hadn't finished carving the stamps yet." I took out a stamp carved with an image of a U.F.O. above a tank driven by a duck and handed it to Nick.

"After you stamp your book, can you stamp the logbook? That way, people can see what the image should look like. There was also an arrow on the back of the stamp showing which way to position it. I pulled my stuff out of the bag and found a log that looked intact enough to perch on. Fall into one decayed log and you learn your lesson. Nick plopped down next to me and arranged his logbook as well.

"So, are you and Trace here together? I saw you arrive while I was walking down by the lake." He stamped the image onto a black ink pad.

I froze. How would Nick know Trace? My mind started throwing worst-case scenarios at me, featuring Nick as a crazed stalker using me to get closer to her. The walk was all a ploy for information. I reigned in my rampant imagination and answered.

"Yup, but she's totally new to 'boxing, so I'm not sure how into it she'll get."

"Oh. That's a shame." I wasn't sure what the disappointment in his voice was from.

"But you are, too," I said.

"Am what?" he asked.

"New to 'boxing."

He tilted his head and looked at me, his forehead wrinkled in confusion. "I think we're talking about two different things."

I waited.

"Are you and Trace here together as a couple?" he tried again.

"Oh!" I was so surprised that I laughed. "No, nope. Not that there's anything wrong with that. I just mean I'm available. I mean, she's available. We are both single and not together. Singularly."

I knew by then I was blushing brighter red than the ink in my hand. Smooth. That's me.

He was polite enough to look down, hide his smile, ignore my discomfort, and go back to the task at hand.

"Fantastic carve on this stamp." He admired the image in his logbook.

I cleared my throat and agreed. It wasn't the first time people had misjudged us as a couple. We'd been friends for so long that we acted like an old married couple, sometimes finishing each other's sentences. I was getting a vibe he was still asking more about my availability.

Nick took the U.F.O. stamp first, inked it with blue ink, and stamped it in his no longer blank, virgin book. After packing everything back up, I left him to re-stack the rocks on top of it, but I did sneak a peek to make sure he did a thorough job so the average hiker wouldn't stumble upon it.

"Next one?" he asked. By then, the awkward teenage flashback moment had passed, and I was happy to be out in the woods with a like-minded person.

"You mentioned getting here earlier. Did you do any hiking near the house next door?" I asked.

"No, but Fisherman talked about heading over there. He said he was eaten alive by mosquitos."

I stopped. "What fisherman?"

"No, as in his trail name is the Fisherman. I think his real name was Ned?"

"Nathan?" I suggested, hoping I was wrong.

"Yeah, that's him. He said he was still going to camp over that way, even after Alice said he could stay at her place. You know him?"

I shook my head and kept walking. What the heck was Creepy Tent Guy Nathan trying? If he was here for the letterboxing event, why didn't he just say so?

Nick read out the next part of the clue. *"Now that you know what is causing the lights and sounds, you're unsure what to do. Should you continue to see what is making the noise in the trees ahead, or should you go back to bed and ignore this entire thing as a bad dream? If you decide to continue, walk until you see a two-in-one tree in the middle of the path."*

"What is a two-in-one tree?" Nick asked.

"It's a tree that splits into two trunks. You'll see that type of clue a lot. Sometimes, there are three or four in one tree."

"Got it. Let's keep going."

The trail widened allowing us to comfortably walk side by side. "Are you staying in town or camping?" I asked.

"Camping over by the herb garden. Alice seems to have quite a green thumb."

"Drat, I hoped you would have duck clues for me," I explained my room.

"Well, you didn't ask if I had a duck clue."

I stopped and turned towards him.

"When I got here, and Alice showed me where to put my tent, she handed me a packet with two mini ducks and a note." He said.

"Alice is awesome." I waited for a heartbeat and then prodded him. "Well? What was on your ducks?"

He looked around, pretending as if seeing if anyone else was nearby. "Does this mean we're going to show each other our ducks?" He grinned. "I had the word Easel."

I wrote his information down in my book and gave him what I had.

"Want to team up on it?" he asked.

"Well, there's only one room up for grabs."

"Yeah, I know." He put his book away and continued down the trail.

I chuckled, enjoying the casual flirtation.

"And that would be my two-in-one tree up ahead." He looked down at his clue. *"The aliens must have damaged this tree and split it down the middle. Search inside to see what they might have used."*

We settled into a comfortable afternoon of finding the rest of the locations and preparing the series for the next day. The last stamp was only a few feet from where the trail ended at the small lake down from the inn. I could see the Inn's Widows Walk through the trees. The trail wasn't a true loop, but you could see the beginning of the trail across the field. A soda can was caught in the reeds at the edge, so I grabbed it to take back with me.

Usually, I carried a trash bag while hiking to pick up stray bits of litter as I went, but I knew Alice and Jason walked this trail often enough that it wouldn't need much maintenance. However, the lake was big enough to touch other properties, and the trash they sometimes shared with the rest of the world made its way over to this side.

From here, I could see the path that would take you to my future home. I'd been compartmentalizing it while doing the clues, but the urge to go back and rummage around in it was overwhelming momentarily. Until the pesticide was cleared, I could only focus on this event. I dragged my brain away from BnB ideas in time to notice we were back on the main lawn.

"Thanks for letting me come along," Nick said as he motioned to a group of tents to our left. "I'm the green and white one if you need help with anything, but I plan on heading into town soon before the bookstore closes. I finished the book I brought with me." A reader on top of everything else. Be still my heart.

I would need to make time to talk to Nick, a.k.a. Green Archer, a bit more this weekend. Walking around the house to the front, I found that all was not as peaceful as I'd left it.

Chapter Seven

The driveway was now packed with cars haphazardly blocking other cars in. Jason was carrying in bags. Alice had sleeping bags in one arm as she escorted an older lady into the house. I spied Trace playing car Jenga, trying to fit cars in after they dislodged their people and baggage. I threw my backpack down out of the way and jumped in to help.

I flagged down Alice. "What the heck is going on?"

"A combination of people showing up that hadn't RSVP'd on the event site mixed with people not having a place to stay thanks to the festival in town." She handed me a printout of who she had where.

"Was I in some time warp or something? How did you organize this all so quickly?"

She shrugged. "It's my superpower."

"Remind me to tap into that when I get my place up and running."

"I cannot <u>wait</u> to help."

I took my paper and started towards the first group, who were standing aimlessly next to a pile of luggage. They were a middle-aged couple, but I could see the spark in their smiles. They were excited about this weekend and not bothered by the chaos.

"Hi, you must be the Lost Gnome and Gamer Geek." Or Chris and Clara in the real world, according to my guide. I recognized them from the selfie that Trace sent from the trail. I hadn't needed to make a massive leap on guessing which was which as Chris had on a shirt with a row of gnomes and Clara wore a shirt that said she'd rather be gaming.

"Looks like you're two of the lucky ones with an actual room instead of a spot in the barn." I offered to grab one of their backpacks and introduced myself on the walk to the house. "My friend Coffee Cat, you've already met, and I'm sure you've met your hosts, Alice and Jason. Feel free to grab any of us if you have any questions about the event."

"Is the duck theme based on your stamp name?" Chris asked.

I shrugged. "Came up from a late, caffeine-filled night surrounded by themed rubber ducks and bad Sci-Fi movies. Alice thought it would be quirky, and we ran with it. Who knew we'd have UFO sightings to add to the weekend's flavor?"

"Looks like someone is waiting for you so we can get ourselves inside." Chris motioned over my shoulder. When I turned to see what he meant, no one was there. It must have been someone tracking clues and happened to be looking our way. Ignoring it,

I pointed them up the stairs to the room at the top right. They would share a wall with me, so I hoped neither were heavy snorers.

In less time than it took most people to make a decision, Alice had everyone sorted and in their proper place. She earned super bonus points by appearing with a tray of assorted, still-warm cookies a few moments later.

"Help yourself," Alice said. "I'm making little plates for each room."

"I can't believe the turnout! And so many early arrivals. I figured most would be here tomorrow."

"It was all pretty last-minute, and it's not like starting things early changes anything."

Around a mouthful of caramel chocolate heaven masquerading as a cookie, I said, "The paintings you added to the room are fantastic."

She blushed slightly, pleased. "I love decorating to a theme, and this one was too fun to pass up. Wait til you see what I do for Halloween!"

"Where did you even get the paintings?

"I went and bought a bunch of paintings at the thrift store and added UFOs and aliens to them. Only took a few minutes, so I put them in all the rooms."

"I had no idea you could paint." I said, grabbing a second cookie.

Alice chuckled. "I haven't done it in a while, but adding those few bits to already finished paintings is easy. A few are blended better than others."

Jason walked by and toted a large telescope up the front stairs.

"Stars going to be good tonight?" I asked.

He set it down to rest on the top stair. "Well..." He appeared embarrassed. "You never know what you'll see."

He picked it back up and kept walking.

"He's probably looking for the UFOs," Nick said as he appeared beside me, holding up the front page of the county paper. 'Locals Spot Moving Lights' was the front page.

Alice held the cookie plate out to him. "Yup, he's all excited about possibly catching sight of a ship. We were meant to have a meteor shower Saturday night, which we should be able to see if the weather report stays clear. There was a thunderstorm during the last meteor shower, and he moped around for days."

"Don't the lights from town cause an issue?" I couldn't help asking.

Alice shook her head. "We're at the best spot for night viewing."

"Well, I appreciate the potential aliens staying on theme for us." I took a final cookie from the tray promising myself I would exercise more. Starting tomorrow.

"Let me deliver a couple of these for you. Wait, so we each have a new painting in our room. Does that mean I need to see what everyone else's painting looks like to solve the clue?"

Alice nibbled on one of her macaroons. "They are enjoyable to look at if I do say so myself." She handed a plate to Nick. "Could you take these outside and put them on the table?"

Watching to make sure he had left, Alice turned to me and whispered. "The paintings are just a red herring." She winked and handed me two plastic wrapped plates.

"Those two plates go to the people in the old butterfly room and the room beside them."

The butterfly room was the first one off the kitchen. I knocked and was greeted with an eyeball, looking out from a crack in the doorway.

"Um. Hi." I presented my friendliest smile and held up the plate. "Alice sent these for you. I'm Rubber Duckie/Remi."

The door opened a crack more, revealing a chubby man with curly black hair wearing jeans and a Teenage Mutant Ninja turtle shirt. I took a leap of faith. "Are you Ninja Turtle?" I asked.

"Yeah." He said, taking the plate from me. "These look good."

I spied one of Alice's paintings over his shoulder. "Do you mind if I come in and look at your painting over the fireplace?"

He looked up at me and then behind him into his room.

"Or if you could take a picture of it and text me?" I asked, seeing he was reluctant.

"No, it's fine." He stepped back, opening the door wider.

I explained how Alice had made them. They may be a red herring, but I still wanted to see them. His painting showed a main street through town with alien creatures mixed in with the regular folks. I scanned the rest of the room, admiring the updates Jason had done. When I first came, the walls were covered by paisley butterfly wallpaper, each the size of a large pizza. It was a psychedelic nightmare with the added visual attack of shag blue carpeting. I half wished I could meet the old owners just to ask them what they were thinking. Now, the walls were a sedate sage green with touches of cream and blue around the room and an herbal motif of flowers and naturalistic silhouettes.

Ninja Turtle stood awkwardly in front of his desk, his body blocking my view of the papers there, the plate still unwrapped and held in his hand.

"Thanks for letting me look. Enjoy the cookies." I ran into Alice in the hallway, still carrying a plate.

"Thanks for delivering them. I just have this last one to take to the kitchen."

"You were too quick. I've missed my chance to snoop in the other rooms now." I said.

"Oh, you never know what might pop up." She smiled but didn't reveal any more. I snagged an oatmeal scotchie from her before she left as an emergency cookie for later. I would definitely only eat salad tomorrow.

A text from the pesticide office let me know the tent was going in place. No more trips were allowed into the house until it was declared safe from fumes. I found the stairs to the widow's walk and went up to see Jason bent over a large telescope aimed over the trees.

"Hey there! Seeing anything?" I asked.

He looked up and shrugged. "Nothing except the alien invasion at your place," he teased. He waved me over to look through the lens. I zoomed in and watched as the team started working on the tarps. I moved it a little over to where Nathan had his tent, but it was gone. Good riddance. I mentally cursed his laziness at the debris he left behind. Not much of a hiker if he didn't follow the "leave no trace" rule.

"At least having it tented like ET's house fits the weekend," I said. "Please text me if you see anything weird out there."

I went back downstairs, curled up on the front porch, and opened the packet from the lawyer. He was right. The offers were significantly more than the house should go for, but that wasn't what surprised me. The second offer was from Alice and Jason. Why wouldn't they have mentioned that? The other one was from a real estate firm. I shoved them both back into my backpack to deal with later. I wasn't selling, but I did have questions.

Instead, I started drawing out a rough house layout based on the little we managed to see. I texted Trace with some layout questions. I knew I wanted to make it a place where people could gather to play games and maybe branch out to geeky crafts. I honestly had no idea if the space would work for it. Any renovations were going to be done by yours truly, so I'd need to carefully plan. The ground level had a large living area. I could envision multiple tables set up there and in what I took to be a formal dining room.

My blood pressure went up a little when Trace didn't respond as quickly as expected, and I realized I hadn't heard from her in a while.

Chapter Eight

In an ordinary world, I wouldn't think twice about Trace not answering right away but hearing about the weird stalker texts had put me on high alert. Now, it's possible she was just out walking. Most of the area had spotty, if no, service. I walked around the house and found Alice near the garden.

"Alice, have you seen Trace?"

"No, when we got back, she helped settle people in. I saw her talking to Zack, oh, um, Night Hiker, and some of the others. I got wrapped up in things here, but I think they were all going out again."

"Which one is Night Hiker?" I asked.

"You can't miss him. Tall blond guy with a beard who hikes in a black kilt."

I realized she was juggling a paperwork-filled clipboard and a coffee. I felt guilty I'd left her to deal with everything.

"Can I help?" I scanned the various groups for Trace's red shirt.

"Not a thing needed, hon. I used to arrange conventions in my pre-farm life. This is a breeze. Clues distributed and sleeping arrangements finalized." She gestured with her clipboard. "This is planning for my next garden plot. Go enjoy yourself!"

People were on a sugar high from her decadent, homemade treats. She was the wonder woman of organization. I was beat from all the running around, but it was too early to crash, and I'd feel better once I found Trace. I decided to see if anyone else wanted to try one of the local mystery boxes with me and check the area for her.

I started walking to the green, striped tent and stopped. No. You will not grab Nick to go letterboxing after you've just gone hiking with him. That seemed like desperation. I spied Russ and Sue relaxing in the rocking chairs on the porch and going through their stamp images.

"You two want to head out with me? I'm going to try the box near the railroad."

"That picture clue posted yesterday?" Russ asked, grabbing his hiking poles and pack.

"Not for me, thanks," Sue declined. "I did that one on my way in."

"Anything we should know about the box?" Sometimes, it's good to get a heads-up about poison ivy or a particularly steep hill.

"Nope."

I waited a beat, but nothing else was offered. "Thanks. By the way, have you seen Trace recently?" I glanced at my phone and saw I was at zero bars. I'd have to find her the old-fashioned way.

"Not since we got back," Russ said. "Didn't you stay with her a bit, Sue?"

Sue looked up from her book, eyes wide. "Me? For a bit. Last I saw, she was huddled up with that guy."

"Zack? Scott?

She shrugged. "I didn't stay long enough to find out. They obviously wanted to be alone. He was all over her." That last bit was said with a sneer.

That didn't sound like Trace at all. And was that a bit of jealousy that the guys were flocking around Trace? I wasn't about to broach it with Russ standing there.

"Anyway, I went to the barn to pack some snacks, and by the time I came out, they were both gone," she said.

"If you see her, could you ask her to check in with Alice or leave me a note?" I asked.

"Yeah, sure," Sue said as if I'd asked her to mop the floor.

I wasn't thrilled to hear Trace was off with some random guy, but I could hardly yell at her after doing the same thing myself. As we started our mini hike, I turned up the volume on my phone so I would not miss any incoming texts. Russ walked with a bit of a limp, so I slowed down my pace to match his.

"Got a bad knee on my right side," he said. "Hope you don't mind going a bit slower."

"Not at all."

"Great little town and woods," he said as we walked. "I'm looking forward to seeing what tomorrow brings. I've been to about four events in the past few months and already have several hundred stamps. There was this one stamp in North Carolina..."

At that point, I realized I had a talker on my hands. There would be no communal silence and enjoying nature on this walk. I was pleased I'd picked a clue with a short walk and just one box. I might survive that long, especially as he seemed happy enough if all I did was listen. Maybe Sue wasn't a good listener.

"Then I was 'boxing in Maryland with the Wallace Twins. Have you ever 'boxed with them? They walked so fast that I had a horrible time keeping up, but we had coffee at this little cat cafe afterward. They'd never seen anything like it. It's nothing like boxing with the Penguin Family..."

As long as I nodded now and again, it appeared my part of the conversation was handled. We got to the last bit of the clue and read that the box would be at eye level in the oak tree five steps from the path. I could see the knot from the trail but left it to him to discover. His eyes lit up as he pointed it out, and I mirrored the look. Finding the box was still a bit like getting a present. You never knew what you would get, but it was a reward for the trip. This particular find had a rubber stamp of a squirrel hiding nuts in a tree. We stamped our carved images in the logbook and put the squirrel image in ours.

Russ used markers to color the tree brown and the leaves green on his image, leaving a second shade of brown for the squirrel. The images in his book were tiny pieces of art. My patience and skill level stuck with an ink pad and a solid color. He offered the stamp to me already inked, so I accepted. While he re-hid the box,

I rechecked my phone, and still no bars. I would have to restrain myself to match his pace and not rush back.

My feet ached, and my body was demanding rest when we were within sight of the front porch. Russ had to slow down for me this time. This was ridiculous. I had to get back into shape. Too much sitting at a desk all day was making Remi a marshmallow. "Thanks for coming with me. I'm going to head in for a bit." I reached into my pocket and pulled out an index card. "Here's a special clue only given out by this piece of paper. After you find the box, feel free to pass it on to someone else."

"I'm heading out right now." He said.

I smiled and waved 'bye. There had been no sign of Trace along the trails. She could have gone into town, but there was a signal there, and she would have received my multiple 'please check in' posts. My call went straight to voicemail, and my texts remained unanswered. Alice had left me one saying she was running into town, so at least I knew the phone worked. I refused to blow this out of proportion. She was fine. The calls were probably some screwed-up prank. Filling my head with happy scenarios of Trace's day, I decided to wait upstairs.

The stairs up to my room loomed like Mt. Everest. I looked at the settee in the foyer and debated collapsing there. It had a pillow. I was short enough to fit. Head down, I began the trek up the two staircases when I was startled by Ninja Turtle's door opening.

As one of the event organizers, there was a moment when I was going to turn and check in with him. Make sure all went well so far. That he was having fun. My body had other plans, so I gave him a brief nod as he scuttled back into his room. Knowing I needed to move before my legs stiffened, I leaned on the banister and worked my way up the stairs. A tiny shred of dignity and stubbornness kept me from getting down on my hands and knees to crawl the final bit.

I knocked on Trace's door, not expecting an answer, so I stood there, not speaking for a moment when she opened the door.

"Remi? Are you okay?" She asked, putting a hand on my shoulder.

"Me?" I said a bit too loudly. "Why haven't you answered me all day?"

She walked into her room and came back holding a phone with a smashed glass on the front. "I tripped and it met a rock it didn't like. I got a ride into town to pick up a new one, and I only got back a few seconds ago. Did something happen?" She looked me over.

"Other than you having a strange person stalking you? People throwing rocks and yelling at me in diners? A young guy dying at your apartment complex? Creepy tent guys sneaking around? A house full of poisonous fumes? Nope, not a thing." I shook my head and took a deep breath. In and Out. "Don't mind me. Tired, stressed and grumpy. But I'd feel a lot better if we checked in throughout the day."

"Done." She nodded. "Don't let this become a bugbear. I'll get my phone up and running, and you go chill."

She knew calling the problem a bugbear would make me smile. We'd overhead someone using that to describe a horrible project they were working on. Around that same time, Trace and I started playing Dungeons and Dragons and discovered that bugbears were a bit more than a nuisance. Unfortunately, both horrible situations and gross monsters fit the phone message issues.

I knew what I needed. Trace safely in her room, I went straight to my luxurious bathroom and started to fill up the tub. It was large enough to take me and at least one other human, so filling it would take a bit. Not that someone to fill that role was in the picture. I threw some muscle relaxer bath bombs in and pulled out the current mystery book I was reading.

How could it be barely after seven? My face erupted into a yawn. Okay, must avoid going near the bed. If I did that, I'd pass out, and the next thing I'd hear was screaming and panic as my bath flooded and made its way down the hallway. I needed to get my blood pumping and back on track for a bit longer, or I'd be wide awake at 3 am.

I knew who I'd like to have come by and get my blood pumping, but I promised myself I wouldn't fall into an immediate rebound. And casual hookups weren't my thing. Even if the way one part of his hair fell into his eyes was adorable. I eased my way down to the wood floor and did some stretches while the bath filled.

Armed with my book and a cold can of Diet Coke, I stayed in the tub until my skin wrinkled and the water got cold. Scrubbed and squeaky clean, I threw on my flannel Pajamas in time to answer the door. I stood back to let Alice in.

"Oh dear, I didn't mean to get you out of bed," she said checking out my duck-themed pajamas.

"I wasn't. I'm in a very zen-like state from that heavenly tub and felt like getting into comfy clothes."

"Isn't that tub wonderful? He installed one in our bathroom, too." She smiled. "You know it can fit two..."

"Um, yes, I can see it would." I said, cutting her off.

She winked and put her hand on my arm to show she was teasing. "Jason and I wanted to invite you and Trace to a late dinner. With everything going on, we never had a chance to eat."

I paused, looking down at my pajamas.

"Oh, come as you are - it's just us. Go to the door on the other side of the kitchen and come on through. We use that for our private dining room." She opened my door to step out, and there was Nick, hand in the air, preparing to knock.

Alice turned to me and winked. "Take your time, hon."

Nick raised his eyebrow as he gave me a quick but obvious up-and-down appraisal. Towel-dried hair and flannel PJs are not the impression I wanted to make on anyone, but then again, I was over pretending to be someone I wasn't. This was me. Take it or leave it.

"I wanted to bring you this." He handed me a stamp carved in the shape of a duck with a black mask and nun chucks. "I found it on the trail earlier."

"Why isn't this in its box? No one would even have these clues yet." I groaned and wondered how I would fix this while simultaneously worried there were other issues with boxes planted over the last month. I had assumed they would still be there and in good condition. There hadn't been storms or anything to dislodge them. "Thanks for bringing it by."

"If you need help getting it back to where it belongs, I'm happy to head out and drop it off."

I looked out the window and saw it was getting dark.

"I've hiked in the dark plenty of times," he said. "Not an issue. Really."

It was probably the only way I would get it done without collapsing. I grabbed my binder, pulled out the clues for the four-stamp collection the Ninja Duck was part of, and gave him a copy. "This one should go in the third box. If you can check on the others, that would be great." I handed him an extra logbook, bags and a container. "If anything needs to be replaced or repaired, please feel free to fix it."

He juggled everything into one hand.

"I really appreciate this," I said.

"I'm on it." Just before he left, he turned back to me. "Should I... come by later tonight and tell you how it went?"

"I'd love to be responsible and say yes, but once I lay down, I'll be out for the night."

"That wasn't exactly a no." He raised an eyebrow and gave a hint of a smile.

"No. Thank you. Please text if there's an issue." I put my hand on his chest and gently pushed him back into the hallway, laughing at the flirtation. Trace opened her door in time to see me inches from him, my hand on his chest

Chapter Nine

"He is awfully adorable, isn't he?" Alice whispered to me at the dining table after Trace regaled them with our hallway meeting. "Kind of like a young Clark Kent. You know, hiding behind those glasses is a yummy..."

"Alice!" I hissed.

My last snack seemed like a millennium ago, and even if I'd been full, the pot roast and potatoes she served would have found room to fit. How did Jason stay so slim with this woman cooking?

I looked over at Trace, about to turn the conversation over to be about her. "Where's your necklace?" I asked, noticing she wasn't wearing her one constant piece of jewelry: a Celtic heart pendant from her parents.

She frowned and reached up out of habit. "The chain broke when I tripped earlier. I couldn't find a replacement in town, so it's in my room."

Alice patted her hand. "I'm glad it's just a broken chain and not lost then."

"Did you know Nick before today?" I asked, casually taking a second dinner roll at the same time. The bowls holding the family-style meal were brightly colored pieces of pottery that were of varying levels of skill. Alice wouldn't throw a perfectly good crafting attempt away if it could be used. Their imperfections increased their charm.

"No," Jason said. "We ran into him while showing Trace the stream that runs behind your place, and he joined us for a bit."

"What was he doing out that way?" I wasn't aware of any boxes on that trail. I guess he could have been hiding one. Or was he using it as a fake coincidence to give him time with Trace? Maybe he wasn't here for letterboxing at all. Or maybe Remi, he just likes to hike. I told myself to be quiet and enjoy the meal.

"Don't know, but he sure seemed interested in you," Trace said as she speared a bit of roast.

I hid my grin behind my glass. Ignoring Trace was the best way to proceed, or she wouldn't stop. I knew this whole teasing about Nick was her way of keeping my spirits up. There had been so much drama in the past year. Now it's time for a fresh start.

Thinking of my place reminded me of the legal packet. Were Alice and Jason waiting for a good time to mention trying to buy the place? Are they waiting for me to bring it up?

Alice beamed at us. "I can't thank you enough for co-running this event with me. So many people staying have already booked to return with their families in the Fall. But even without that, having you two as friends has been worth it."

We clinked our glasses in a 'cheers' and settled into the meal. It was Alice, Jason, Trace, and I, as the inn didn't provide dinners. We were eating as a family. Something Trace and I never had much outside of each other.

"How much more work do you still need to get done before you can be an Inn officially?" I asked, debating if I could manage another bite.

"Jason's working on the last guest bedroom, and it should be done by next month at the latest. We have some supplies on back-order that have held things up."

"After that, it's clean-up work and some of Alice's decorative touches to finish," he said.

"You mean the UFO paintings aren't staying up?" I feigned shock.

Jason and Alice laughed. "No, I was going to give them out if people wanted them." Trace and I both raised our hands and said in unison.

"Me! Me!"

"It can go next to your dinosaur head," Trace agreed.

My last boyfriend required our house to be designer-perfect, and to me, it always felt like I was living in a cold demo house with no feeling or character. So, when I moved into my apartment, I went bold. Walls of blue, green, and red. Beige and eggshell were dead to me, even if it meant losing a security deposit. Trace commissioned an oversized painting to hang over my fireplace of Rubber ducks attacking a city. From that, my eccentric collection grew. I had a resin dinosaur head on one wall as a 'trophy,' multi-colored lanterns hanging down from the ceiling, and a large art piece made of upcycled dead books. My personality was aggressively stamped all over that place.

"What do you think about goats?" Jason asked Alice.

I stopped in mid-bite at the abrupt change of topic.

"Well, dear. I can't say, as I've given goats much thought during a normal day," she replied.

"I was reading up on them in this month's EcoJournal. They're great for keeping the yard manicured and could be good for kids to pet."

I shoved food into my mouth, but Jason turned and asked me my opinion anyway.

"Well, I love being around animals, but you already have such a fantastic site here. If you had goats, you'd have, well, goat poop all over the lawn. That would be a hard sell for the wedding business. Maybe there are other ways to keep moving towards 'going green'?" I said, keeping my attention on my plate for a minute.

"Excellent thinking," Alice said. "I hadn't even considered the wedding trade yet."

"Remi, your place would be fantastic to host a wedding, too," Trace said around a mouth half-full of pie. "Can you imagine the photo opportunities alone with a long, royal gown and the turrets in the background? Where else will they get something like that on the East Coast?

I shrugged. "That may be putting the cart before the goat. We still have the tenting to get through. After that, it'll be a hot mess for a while." I steeled myself and turned to Alice. "So, it seems people are interested in buying the place from me."

Jason blushed. "We put that in before we knew it was you, Remi. I doubt you're interested in selling, but if you are, please think of us first. We don't want some developer buying up the place and destroying the area around her."

I raised my glass of water to them both. "Deal." Relief melted the tension in my shoulders I hadn't realized was there.

I turned to Alice. "What about you two? Weddings here?"

Alice tilted her head in thought. "We've advertised as a family-friendly escape focused on nature. I'll look into the wedding side. I'll also need to make sure that doesn't require some other permit we need to deal with. Getting this place approved through the town council is taking long enough."

I stopped chewing. "Permits and zoning, oh joy." The dread of dealing with bureaucracy made me lose my desire for pie.

"We can help you through the process," Jason offered.

"And I'm happy to help research wedding venue offerings," I offered. "Research is my thing, after all."

"Not to jinx it, but what about your plans for next door?" Jason asked.

"Totally different thing. A BnB for gamers, but also focus on having groups for gaming sessions that don't require overnight stays. I think there might be a monthly membership fee to come in and access all the board games. A cat café and coffee bar." I nodded towards Trace on that bit. "For the overnight guests, we'd do something like a three-day role-playing game tournament or something similar to your letterboxing gathering." I couldn't leave that poor last bite of pie alone on the plate. "We'd be great for each other's overflow when needed, and I could offer a day pass or something for your guests."

"And we could offer the farm experiences for yours!" I could see the wheels in Jason's head turning.

I would add that to the notebook full of ideas I'd been keeping. Sated and warm from the company, I found my eyelids closing of their own accord. My body was sending firm signals that enough was enough. We'd gone full speed for almost fourteen hours, and I was done. Tomorrow, things would start in full force.

Chapter Ten

Stretching, I enjoyed the feel of slightly achy muscles, knowing they were well-earned. I woke easily, knowing it was the first day in forever that I could remember being well-rested and content. Spending the evening with friends and good food was the best soul-healing medicine a person could ask for.

I was ready for a new start to clean out all the post-breakup garbage from my head and find my path forward. I'd done the obligatory junk food eating and movie watching with Trace, who wisely never once uttered the dread 'I told you so' phrase. I wallowed, unbathed for the weekend, and then decided he wasn't worth it. The person I thought he was didn't exist, and I was mourning the loss of a fictional character. Time to move on.

I jumped into the shower, threw my hair in a wet ponytail, and grabbed a fresh pair of shorts and a T-shirt. The weatherman said high nineties today.

Trace opened the door to my room after an obligatory brief announcement knock. "Better get a move on, Ducky. The natives are up and ready to hunt."

"Hey! What if I was in the middle of getting dressed or something?" I asked.

"Well then, I would tell you to throw something on and stop being a lazybutt."

I grabbed the two tote bags of assembled clue packets and counted. "I hope we have enough for everyone." People who hadn't registered had shown up all day yesterday. What if more came today?

Trace went into her room and came back with a large legal envelope filled to bursting.

"I wave my magic wand, and voila!" She opened the clasp to reveal bundles of paper-clipped clues. "When I helped with the printing job, I went a little print happy. Brought these just in case. They won't be as themed as your packets, but they'll at least have the clues."

Boy Scouts had nothing on her. "My hero!" I tucked them into my tote bags. "Now, let's get some caffeine and start this thing."

"Hold a sec. Gotta take this," she said, answering her phone.

There's nothing worse than only hearing half a conversation that starts with "the man that died" to a bunch of "nos." I watched her face as her eyes widened and her jaw dropped. She hung up and looked at her phone for a second.

"I swear, if you don't tell me right now what that was about, I will hit you with that pillow." I mock threatened, trying to break her out of her odd stupor.

"That was the police. That guy who died in the apartment? He had photos of me thumbtacked to his wall. A crazy amount of photos. They wanted to know if we were dating. I need to go to the station next week."

"What? You didn't even know him."

She looked up at me. "Do you think the phone calls could have been from him?" She absentmindedly started chewing on her fingernail. I hadn't seen her do that for years. "I swear I can't even remember ever having a full conversation with him. I just don't understand."

She was spiraling. I put the box down and pulled her in for a hug. "Look, I'm sure a lot was going on with him. This is not on you. Did the police have anything to say about it?"

Trace pulled back and shook her head. "They only wanted to know how well I knew him and what issues we had. Oh my god, they must consider me a suspect."

"Okay, stop." I said firmly. "Do you want to stay up here today, and we can watch movies or something?"

"Remi, you have a crowd of people waiting for you."

"And I would bail in a minute if you needed me here."

She rested her head on my shoulder for a moment before straightening up and squaring her shoulders. "Let's do this thing."

I peeked out the front window downstairs to see how many people were up and about. My casual perusal stopped when I spied a familiar tent on the far left. Thankfully, my tea mug was only about an inch from the table when I let go.

"Trace!" She must have heard the slight hint of hysteria in my voice because she hoofed it over to the window.

"What? What?"

"Do you know who is staying in that tent?" I asked.

She shook her head and did a slight shrug. "Sorry, I haven't been paying attention to who is staying where. Why? Talk to me."

"That blue tent next to the begonias was last seen in my storage locker."

"Tents all look alike to me. Is it possible you're…"

"Don't. Even. Say, I'm imagining it. That white splotch on the side is from me spilling paint." I turned her to look toward the tent as a brunette, compact man stepped past the tent flap.

"Bob!" We said in unison. Turning to face each other, we both showed a mixture of annoyance and dismay. "What is Bob doing here?"

"Wow, you two said that in stereo," Sue broke in, joining us in the kitchen. "That's Chef Bob. He said this was his first event."

"And his last," Trace muttered. I grabbed my bag and hurried to keep up as she stormed out the door.

My scheming ex looked up and must have seen enough on Trace's face to have him open the tent flap wider for a smaller person to come out. His ten-year-old nephew, Sean. Of course, he brought his nephew as a shield from two angry women. Trace paused, took a deep breath, and seemed to struggle to adjust her expression to one of frozen welcome as she approached them.

"Hi, Sean," I fist-bumped Sean, only giving Bob a minute nod of acknowledgment. "I think some boys are around the house playing football. Why don't you see about joining?"

He took a moment to get the okay from Bob before jogging away from the rising tension with the adults.

"It's good to see you, Remi." He tilted his head towards me and ignored Trace. "Sean learned about letterboxing in Boy Scouts and asked if I'd bring him. What brings you two here?" He smiled with all dimples and innocence.

"I'm running the event, as you bloody well know." My arms crossed, I waited to hear the lies.

He looked back at me. "No, but it's a pleasant surprise." He put his hand on my arm, staring into my eyes as if nothing existed in the world but me.

The look would have at one time made me purr like a kitten, but now his manipulations made me cold.

"How the blooming heck did you get this tent?" I growled.

"The unit is still in both our names. I didn't think you'd mind me borrowing it when it's for Sean."

"It may be in both names, but it's not like you ever paid a bill. Besides, this is hardly the first time you've taken things from me without asking, is it? Speaking of which, where is Baron?" I would have one hundred percent preferred to see my Australian Shepherd rather than Bob.

"I wasn't sure if dogs could come, so I got him a great dog sitter."

We were drawing attention, and I needed to get things going. "I'll be sure to remove the rest of my things from storage and close out the account when this is done. You can stay, for Sean's sake."

Trace leaned in closer to him. "This isn't done. You leave Remi alone," she warned.

I turned around with my back to him and walked towards the rest of the people starting to gather. I took a few calming breaths on the way. I didn't know what he was playing at, but with Bob, it was always some con or another. This was going to be my relaxing weekend, despite him. Granted, the joyous addition of having Bob wasn't ideal, but I wouldn't let him ruin things. Well, he'd already ruined things when he emptied my bank account for his last hair-brained get-rich-quick scheme, but I wasn't going to let him derail my post-breakup recovery.

I stepped back onto the covered porch and waved to get everyone's attention. "Hi, all! Welcome to the Rubber Duck Invasion! If I could have your attention for a few bits of info before I set you loose on the trail?" My notes were on the clue pile with starred bullets next to the important bits.

"The town of Irving has been overwhelmingly welcoming to us. Volunteers have opened up several of their historic buildings for our use. There's one letterbox in each location. Please, no more than one group at a time in each. The last entrance into a town building is 5 p.m." I paused for a minute and held up one of the clue packets. "I have it all on the front page of the packets I'm giving out. And, of course, there are a bunch of stamps on the local trails that are already posted." No one seemed to have a question, so I continued. "There are a total of 45 event stamps to find this weekend. If you find them all, come see me, and you'll get the Mother Duck Ship special stamp. Come get your clues."

Trace grabbed a bunch of folders and started a separate line of folks to help clear them out faster.

Nick hung back until most everyone had come up.

"Feel ready to head off on your own?" I teased. I noticed the stamp image he put on the event poster. It was of a bow and arrow inside of a TV set. "Was Green Archer a TV show?"

He shrugged. "Sorta. It's an old video game I used to play in college, and my character was the Green Archer. It was the first thing I thought of when trying to come up with a letterboxing name."

I smiled. "If you like games, you'll have to come by when I get my place up and play sometime."

"Wouldn't miss it." He winked.

"My cell number is written inside the folder." I realized what that sounded like. "So if you need me. For trail help. You have my number." I knew I was blushing and couldn't do anything about it. I'd love to know at what age my brain would stop acting like a teenager when a cute guy was around.

"That's her normal number as well." Trace pointed out, giving me a big toothy grin.

"Thanks, I'll be sure to keep it handy." He smiled and went to a nearby spot on the grass to review his clues. Yes, I was rusty, but he was definitely flirting. But was he flirting in interest, or was it just his personality? I hated games. Well, that kind of game. I hated that living with a con artist for three years had made me so distrustful.

Speaking of games, from the corner of my eye, I could tell Bob was staring at me. If he thought I would play some jealousy ploy with him, he didn't know me too well. He could feel what he wanted.

He walked up to me. "Who was that guy you were talking to?"

"Why? You know what?" I waved my hand, shooing him away. "I don't care why. If you want to meet him, he's right over there." I turned away from Bob to smile at Sean as he approached. "Hey bud, are you enjoying camping?"

"Yeah, we explored off-trail a bit yesterday and found a cool old house."

I wondered if he meant "my" house, but that was information I wasn't ready to share within Bob's earshot. Trace continued giving Bob a cold, silent stare. He silently acknowledged he wasn't welcome by turning away. She fulfilled her role as best friend well. Hopefully, not so well that she decided to use her defense skills on him for simply existing. I wasn't against that as a possibility if Sean wasn't around. I wondered if I could find a way to keep Bob away from me. I had a friend at the police academy who might have some advice. Oh my god, Karen. Why hadn't I thought of her before? She would be great to ask about the Trace problem. She was from this area and could hopefully encourage the local office to help.

"Great," said Sean. "Come on, Uncle Bob. Let's go start with the Invasion series." As they walked away, I realized Trace's icy stare was now focused like a laser beam on me.

"Did you tell him about the house?" she asked.

"No! Of course not. I don't know what his deal is, but yes, you have my permission to slap me upside the head if I look like I'm getting back together with him."

I knew she wouldn't. She'd let me make my mistakes and hold my hand afterward while I dealt with the pain, but the promise made her smile. "I'm more worried he's involving Sean in whatever his deal is." Bob was no role model.

"Yeah, we'll keep an eye on him. You focus on the event. But first," she picked up her own clue packet. "I believe Zack is waiting on me to join him on a search for the duck army."

"Back with him today? No, Scott?" I teased. "I never asked how all that went?"

She laughed, ignoring the implication that she may have other reasons than letterboxing to hang out with Zack. "Scott was fine. After he realized my answer was "no," he seemed to just want to be out on the trail. He wanted to know all about letterboxing and may use it in his trail business. Enough about him! I can't wait to find more boxes. I should have gone out with you all those other times.

"Hooray! A convert!" I said, letting her slide on not answering about Zack.

Trace jumped a little as her phone rang.

Chapter Eleven

Trace handed me her phone without checking to see who was calling. "If it's the police again, I just can't."

I held the phone up to her, showing her it was listed as "spam." I was about to return it when a text displayed on the screen.

No ponytail today?

Trace read the text over my shoulder. "Remi, yesterday was the first day in forever that I wore my hair in a ponytail." She hugged her arms to herself.

I wrapped her in a hug. "Okay, let's not jump to assumptions." I needed to think fast. "This doesn't mean the person has seen you today, right? It could still be based on yesterday. Your hair was already up when I picked you up at the apartment, right?"

A pause. "Yeah, just put it up straight from the shower. Once the ambulance came, I didn't bother going back into style or anything."

"So, even though it can't be the guy from below you, it could still be from someone back there and not here. Maybe some creep with nothing better to do than text random strangers?" I gave her a moment to think about it. "Have you given your personal cell number at the wildlife rehab?"

"No!" Her eyes grew wide. "But, remember, I put the flyer for my missing bike on the bulletin board and used my cell phone number." Her shoulders dropped a little with release. "Whew. Okay, so if he texts again, I'll try to talk with him. This could be some teenager trolling me for all we know."

I nodded to show support and keep her calm, but my calm was deteriorating. Neither one of us believed this was harmless. It also didn't explain the photo of her in town yesterday. I remembered to send a quick text to Karen, asking for advice. Even the shyest person would be able to manage a bit more than constant silent phone calls and a threat of "I've been watching you" hidden in a photo.

She looked towards the side of the house, where I saw a man in a kilt, obviously waiting but keeping a polite distance while we talked.

"Right. Is it just you and Zack?" I nodded towards him.

"Just us," she said. I could tell from the slight grimace that she realized a larger group was best.

I had to think quickly. Zack looked more like an accountant than a crazed stalker, but his looks didn't mean anything. I'd feel more comfortable sending Trace off with an armed guard.

"There is something you two could do for me." I waved him over. "Hey, Zack. I'm a little worried about how well the clues in town will go. This is the first time I've tried having a letterboxing combined with stores and people helping. Would you mind starting there with Trace and keeping me updated?"

"As long as it's good with you?" he asked, looking at Trace.

Trace shrugged. "Wherever you want us to start, 'O Fearless Duck Leader,'" she joked. I could see the tension go out of her eyes.

I showed them where the town clues started in the packet. This way, she'd be in public, with good cell phone reception all day.

"Have a great time. Remember to donate to the volunteers!" I yelled after them.

I stopped and looked around, amazed that the ten minutes of chaos had turned into a quiet array of people sprawled on the lawn, planning their routes while others hopped in their cars to head out for the day. It was weird that I only knew about four of them from the trail and postings on the event webpage. Still, for the most part, I'd kept to myself since starting the hobby, so this was all a bit overwhelming. I had thought it would be a small way to do my first event. I did it. Three months of carving stamps, writing fun duck-related clues with Alice, and hiding everything culminated in this.

A heavenly plate was waved in front of me, full of mini banana pancakes covered in syrup and a dollop of whipped cream. "Alice, that looks fantastic."

She smiled. "I made a plate for Trace, too, but I hadn't realized you would both be up and out so quickly. I need someone other than Jason to give feedback on the breakfast options I'm trying out."

I took the plate and followed her to sit on the porch, loving the smell of her flowers lining the front. I wondered if I could get breakfasts from her for my guests. Cooking was not my forte.

"Trace dragged me out of bed to start 'boxing. Everyone was full of energy on the first day of the event. Tomorrow, you might catch a few people sleeping in." I said as I dug into the pancakes, making thankful mmmm noises, but my mind was still on Trace, Bob, the house, and every other random thought my brain threw at me.

"Did I ever tell you I was a therapist before we moved out here?" Alice asked.

Startled out of my daydreaming, I asked. "Do you miss it?"

"Some of my patients, yes." She smiled and put her hand on my arm. "I mainly wanted you to know I'm a good listener."

I put my fork down and looked at her. "Is it that obvious?"

She patted my hand. "Did you and Trace get into a fight or something? Is that why she left?"

I grimaced and took another bite. "I would much rather it had been that." Normally, I was a private person and kept my problems to myself. But before I knew it, I'd filled her in on Trace's stalker, the dead guy, and Bob conning me out of my money and my dog, and now showing up here. By the end, the pancake was history, and I was talked out. The front and side yard being covered in tents, but no people gave me an odd sense of loneliness.

"Oh, honey, that is horrible. I will talk to Jason and make sure he keeps an eye out for Trace as well. I know the Sheriff. Don't let his grumpy demeanor fool you. He's a solid person and he will take your worries seriously."

"Thanks, Alice. I feel better knowing other people will be watching." I pushed away from the table, ready to take my plate into the kitchen. "My other plan was to post a note that told people to text me what Trace was doing every hour for a chance at a special stamp. I don't have a stamp, and Trace would kill me if I did that, but I'm desperate."

"Just leave that, hon." She looked at the plate. "Don't you need to get out there and take care of things?"

"My part is done unless someone texts me for help. What I wanted to do was go next door and explore, but I was told going into the tented home meant certain death. So that's a bit of a deterrent. Maybe I'll head into town. That way, I can be near Trace and pop into the clerk's office to learn about business permits." I slung my bag crosswise across my back. "Anything I can grab for you while I'm in town?"

"If you have the time, you could find the three ducks that escaped." Alice slipped me a folded piece of paper.

"Where did this come from?" I asked. I skimmed it and saw it was a clue story of three alien ducks that decided to leave the mother spaceship and stay on Earth.

"Trace carved the stamps, and Jason and I hid them and wrote the clues." She seemed a little unsure of herself. "We wanted you to have some 'boxing fun this weekend, too. Trace had mentioned things had been rough for you, but I had no idea how rough."

I stood up and gave her a bear hug. "You are the best. I can't wait to get these guys." I felt teary-eyed at the gesture, so I cleared my throat and looked down at the clues. They were an incredible couple, and I was lucky to have met them.

Most of the clues had people at local parks and other hiking trails. The groupings in town were the ones I tried to segment up a bit so each historic building wouldn't be overwhelmed with people. When I pulled in, I was pleased to see a small group of five at the bank stop. The side story was that one duck evaded capture and disguised himself in his human suit to go rob a bank for our currency. He then tried to hop the first train that came into town but was captured and thrown in jail. They could find any of the stamps without going in order, so they didn't have to wait too long, and the three buildings formed a triangle at the end of the parking lot. You could easily see who was at the next clue location and give them time to finish.

The one in the bank was my favorite. The boxers had to solve the clues to figure out the safe combination. The stamp was on a pedestal in the safe as their reward.

I waved to one of the volunteers manning the buildings and got a thumbs-up. I took that to mean the first group donated well.

Hampford's Toy Museum was my next stop, and it was near where my clues from Alice started. A sliver of fear hit me when I saw the ambulance outside the museum. The second day of coming upon ambulances was not good for my stress level. The Toy Museum would have been Trace's first stop.

I pulled to the side of the road, parked illegally, and ran towards the back of the ambulance, where I was stopped by a hulk of a man. His uniform was snug, but due to muscles and not flab.

"Ma'am, there is nothing to see here. Please move away."

I craned a bit to try and see past him. "What happened? Who was it? We're having an event in town this weekend, and I want to check there's no one from my group." I then found myself unable to stop babbling. "Not that if it were, it's more important than some other victim."

"Ma'am, you're going to need to move your car, and please keep this area open."

I smiled at the nice deputy, backing slowly towards my car while trying to find a way to sneak past him. Part of me knew I wasn't being rational. There was no reason to assume it was Trace, but I would feel a heck of a lot better when it was confirmed it wasn't.

Chapter Twelve

Moving my position, I could see the back of a mud-splattered VW Bug way too close to the side of a building. Unless it was some new accordion model, the front end had smashed into the side. Bits of shattered windshield surrounded it. No large, white pillow, so no airbags for cushion. Past the ambulance, I could see a portion of the lump on the gurney, noting the size and shape.

Even covered, it was far too large to be Trace. I let out the breath I was holding. I was going to end up on blood pressure medicine by the end of this weekend.

"Ah, man. Karma sucks, but I'm glad Scott's okay." I looked at the guy standing next to me who had spoken. His shirt read 'Gary, Pest Control.'

"Sorry, a friend of yours?" I asked.

He shrugged. "Friend's a strong word. Most people around town know who he is."

"Why?" I prodded, hating that more information wasn't being volunteered. "He owns half the town? Stays too long at the bar? Raises emus as a hobby?"

He looked at me strangely. I got that a lot. "He's a local hiking guide. A little bit handsy with the ladies, but enough found him charming that he's made a few enemies out of husbands."

"Hiking? Red hair?" I asked, remembering the guy from the diner. "Yeah, that's him."

"Huh, I mean, he was irritating but harmless." If I planned to settle into town, I should start to get to know the people. Gary didn't seem to be hurrying to head back to his truck. I figured there could be only so many pest control businesses in town. "Are you working on that tented house?"

He nodded.

Verbose he was not. "Do you know if we'll be able to get in there before the end of the weekend? I know the timeline says Sunday, but sometimes it ends up being done sooner?" I ended with a question. "Maybe?"

"Nope, Sunday is it. No matter how many times I'm asked."

I waited in case he wanted to tell me about the process or chat, but we stood in silence for a few moments before I gave up. I texted Trace to let her know to skip this area this morning. It was most definitely also an excuse to see how she was doing. Her perfect response was a grinning selfie of her eating a chocolate alien head with Zack, Chris, Clara, Russ, and Sue in the background.

At the same time, a text from Karen popped up asking if Trace had filed a report with the local police at home on the odd texts.

They could see who the calls were coming from. I didn't want to put a damper on her afternoon, but I made a mental note to get that done.

The car crash wasn't near where the alien lab stamp would be, but it was close enough to be awkward. The last thing I wanted was to be pulled in for questioning because I inspired fifty people to tramp around an accident scene. Though with it being a car accident, I wasn't sure what they would do about it. The building wasn't damaged, and no other cars were involved. I couldn't figure out what would have caused him to go that much out of control.

To be safe, I moved the stamp and sent a text out to all contacts listed. I drove back down to the bank area and passed the word along. After finishing up what I could do for the event, I decided to take some time for myself. Permits could wait. I needed to cheer up and not adult for an hour or two.

I pulled out my clue from Alice and Trace and confirmed I was starting at a park on the North end of town. A quick pat of my pocket reassured me the pepper spray was still there, and I groaned. Two pepper sprays. Dang nabbit. I forgot to give Trace one. Okay, she was with a group, and I'd remember tonight. That was why I needed a notebook to keep track of things.

'Cell phone is charged. Check. Water and whistle. I am set.' I carried safety basics when I was out somewhere new and alone. Complete overkill for the quaint little park with a gazebo, but best to keep good safety habits going.

The clue was written as if we were the little ducks exploring the area, and I played along, happy to act like a kid for a bit. Part of me wanted to go back to stare at my house, but no one was going in there without a full hazmat suit any time soon. For now, it was the park.

The clue said the youngest duck tried out the swings at the town's playground, and so did I. I could have skipped ahead to where it said to count forty steps past the water fountain, but what fun was that? When I saw kids heading towards the swings, I relinquished my seat and started my search in earnest. I started again as if walking normally and counted until I reached 40. A little to my right was a giant oak tree. I probably swerved a little as I walked. I went behind the tree and saw an unnatural piling of sticks and rocks. I moved a few aside and saw a bit of Tupperware peeking through.

The stamp image was a cartoon duck hiding behind a rock. I proudly inked the stamp and pressed the image in my logbook.

I watched across the street as some people with paper in their hands tried not to be obvious about what they were doing. I racked my brain and remembered one of the original town stamps was hidden behind a store a few more blocks down. I got up, planning to give them a hint, when I spied Bob chatting with Nathan. He sure seemed to keep popping up for someone who was spending a night camping on his way on a long hike. I crept up along the side of the stone building as if looking for a stamp to hear what they were saying. How would those two even know each other? Before I could get close enough, Bob shook his hand farewell and ran right into me.

"Hey!" I bent down to pick up my backpack I'd dropped in the collision.

"Sorry, luv, I didn't see you there."

I stepped back away from him. "Who was that guy?" I asked, putting my pack on more securely.

"Nate? Great guy. We were in the same extreme frisbee league for a while. Why?"

"Extreme frisbee my Aunt Betty. The only thing you've ever done with sports is bet on it. And your old pal just happened to show up in this little town today." I stared at him in disbelief. "He was being very creepy around Trace."

"I'm sure it was a misunderstanding."

I bristled at the condescending tone. Bob took my hand in both of his. "Let's go somewhere and talk." His thumb stroked the back of my hand.

"Unless you have the money or the dog you stole, we are done chatting." I yanked my hand free and walked around him to continue down the sidewalk, wondering where Nathan had gone. I had no idea if I was going in the right direction for my next clue, but it was away from Bob. After a few minutes of anger induced power walking, I slowed and took the clue out. Oooooh. It was almost like they knew I would have a rough day. My next stop took me to the ice cream store. Yes, please force me to eat homemade goodness.

"Ducks prefer fruitcake-flavored cotton candy scoops in a waffle cone," I told the man behind the counter.

"With duck sauce?" he asked, keeping to the clues script.

"Only on Tuesdays."

He winked, handing me a small box and proper ice cream without duck sauce. Nestled in the box was my last stamp of the day; a spy duck with glasses and a trench coat.

I grabbed a marshmallow threatening to slide off my ice cream, and popped it into my mouth. Cone in hand, I drove back to the inn to check in with everyone. Parking at the house, I decided to walk the garden while I finished my cone. When I turned the corner, I tripped. My ice cream cone dropped from my hand and onto a dead man.

Chapter Thirteen

Finding a strange man lying dead in the pansies may have cured me of ever eating ice cream again. Dead. The skeptic in me wrapped my mind in denial. I couldn't believe it was real, but a small corner of my brain knew he was gone. Living things didn't look that way.

"Um, hello?" I whispered, hoping for an answer. "Sorry about the ice cream." I slowly bent down and moved the melting glob from his back to the ground. I wiped my hand on my pants. He still hadn't moved, so I nudged the body with my foot. Blood had pooled underneath him onto a stepping stone, oozed to the side, and stained my favorite tennis shoes.

I didn't scream, but not due to being fantastic in a crisis. My old college psych classes came to mind and informed me that I'd entered some form of shock. I couldn't think of what to do. My mind focused on everything other than what was in front of me. The sage plant had thrived under Alice's care. I found myself visualizing walking into the inn as if nothing had happened. I could mention it in passing. What were the chances of running into this many bad accidents in the space of a week? I'll go in, have some drinks, and oh, by the way, does anyone know the dead person outside? Should I check for a pulse? Should I scream?

All these thoughts were racing through my head as I stood there, frozen. Maybe if I left and came back, the body would be gone like in one of those wacky murder comedies.

"You lost?" Nick shouted as he came up behind. "Holy--what did you do?"

"Do?" My voice rose a couple of octaves. "I didn't <u>DO</u> anything." I could speak in capitals when very upset. "I was going to sit on the bench, and there he was." I guessed my deer-in-headlights reaction saved me at least explaining that much.

"Stay there, I'll get help."

Oh, good. One of us knew what to do. Although I wasn't sure, I would have chosen the role of staying with the dead person. Oh my God. What if they all thought I did it? Wasn't the person who found the body always the first suspect? But no, I had been around people all day. Hadn't I? My brain was fizzling on its way to a total shutdown. Should we order pizza tonight? No one's going to be cooking. I barely noticed when the police finally arrived, ushering me to the living room with the others.

"Who was it? No one is telling us anything." Trace asked, sitting next to me on the couch. I was wrapped up in a light blanket cocoon and drinking some hot chocolate with a splash of something alcoholic. Outside, the weather may be set for shorts and sandals, but I needed to be wrapped in warmth. The downstairs living room had become filled with people who were on-site during the day, waiting their turn to be interviewed by the police.

"Scott." Saying his name made it finally seem real. I don't see how he even got out of the hospital so quickly after the accident he was just in. Much less..." I waved my free hand vaguely towards the garden.

"Him? Oh, no." Trace folded her arms against her. "He tried talking to me again before we got to the Toy Museum. I blew him off."

"Do you think he was following you?" There was no reason to think he could be the phone stalker, but it seemed suspicious.

Before we could talk more, I was summoned to meet with the Sheriff.

Chapter Fourteen

Despite looking like a mall Santa on steroids, Sheriff Aidan Marrow's sheer existence in front of me made me nervous. I was not getting ho-ho-ho vibes. I'd always been a good girl. Except for that brief time in college, but college never counted, right? I returned my library books on time, paid my taxes, and waited for the walking signal before crossing the road. It was not as if there was a skeleton in my closet. He did just find me with a dead guy who I'd sort of, maybe, threatened recently.

Sheriff Marrow leaned back in the leather office chair. Jason had turned over the library for questions. The Sheriff's eyes trained on me as I rifled through my vast stores of trivial knowledge to remember everything I could about body posture. Don't cross your arms, or you'll appear defensive. Sit relaxed yet alert. While he allowed me a few more minutes to squirm, his eyes traveled around the room, stopping above my head.

'Breathe,' I reminded myself. 'In and out. You're innocent, and this is a routine procedure.'

"Alright, Ms. McKenna, why don't you start from the beginning and tell me what happened."

"Okay. I came back to the inn to see if things were okay, but I wanted to finish my ice cream first. Because it was starting to drip, you know? And I didn't want to have it drip in the house, and I remembered there was this cute bench in the garden." I paused, and he continued to stare at me. "So I went that way and tripped. Over him."

"Did you touch anything?"

"No. Oh, wait. I sort of nudged him with my foot," I admitted.

"I see. Any idea why his shirt was covered in ice cream?"

I noticed a stray rainbow sprinkle clinging to my hand. "Oh, so I dropped it when I fell. And then I think I moved the ice cream off his back? But that's it. Those three things were all I did."

"Did you recognize him?" He idly played with a pen in his hand while he talked.

"Not at first. But yes, my friend Trace and I ran into him at the diner when we got into town. Well, we didn't run into him with like a car." I winced, realizing what I had said. "I mean, we were there. And he was there at the same time. At the diner," Yup, nervous babbling. Innocent people do that.

"And did you talk with him?"

"No, I mean yes, but not really." I winced.

Sheriff Marrow got that look on his face that I often see with people running out of patience with my roundabout answers.

"Okay, so we were there eating, and he, Scott, came over and barged into our conversation. We tried to get him to leave and then he tried to get handsy with Trace."

"And did having Mr. Nelson hit on your friend upset you?" He asked in a tone that implied he would completely understand if it had put me into a murderous rage.

"Of course. He was being a rude jerk who thought our world should stop because he graced us with his presence."

He arched an eyebrow at me, and I felt all the blood going to my cheeks, realizing what I'd said. "Obviously, I wouldn't hurt someone for interrupting a conversation. I only meant that I was annoyed. It's not like he had a chance of getting Trace, so he was just wasting our time."

"How are you so sure Trace wasn't interested?"

"I have eyes?" I sighed, realizing this was going nowhere. "She has been my best friend for years. If Trace had wanted him to stay, she would have said so and not turned her back on him. And Scott's nothing like her type. He left us muttering some snide remark about being able to do better and stomped off to have some temper tantrum about how manly he was."

"You seem to hold a great deal of anger towards the victim." He said.

I took a deep breath. Annoyance overtook discomfort. "I don't hold a thing toward him, about him, over him, or near him. The worst that would have happened was wasting my pie as I threw it in his face if he'd said some of that loud enough for Trace to hear. That's pretty much as violent as I get." I knew my voice was rising, and I started to gesture with my hands, but I couldn't help it. Stumbling across a dead body threw off my day.

He ignored my outburst and continued with his calm questioning. "Was there anyone else at the diner?" he asked.

"The place was packed. I mean, that's why we stopped there. We made it a point to go to whatever the packed local joint was for food. Locals always know best." I shrugged.

"When did you see Mr. Nelson after leaving the diner?"

I got up and started pacing back and forth, trying to work off the excess energy. "Not until about an hour ago when this whole mess started."

"Did you or Ms. Cooper meet up with him at his apartment later that night?"

My forehead creased, confused. "I didn't know where Scott lived. I wouldn't have time to work if I chased down everyone who tried to hit on Trace. Or eat. It wasn't a big deal. Scott even went out hiking with Trace later that same day, and all seemed good."

"You didn't arrange to meet him, knowing everyone was in town?" He continued to prod.

"No! I never saw him again." My face belied the lie as soon as I realized I'd told it, and his keen eye picked up on it as well. "Other than, of course, seeing him loaded into the ambulance after his car crash."

He quirked an eyebrow at me. "You were at the scene of the crash? How long prior to that were you in the area?"

"I was nearby at the old bank and then drove to the museum next. It wasn't too long." I admitted.

"I see. And where were you last night?"

"Here. I had dinner with the innkeepers, and we stayed up pretty late chatting about some ideas for the future. After that, I was fast asleep. It was at least midnight by then. Check my car. If the parking lot is anything like it was earlier, I wouldn't be able to get my car free without getting a whole bunch of people together and playing musical cars to get mine out. Besides, the event started at seven a.m., and I needed to make sure I got some sleep."

"And was Ms. Cooper with you?"

"Yes, it was me, Trace, Alice, and Jason."

He leaned forward. "I need you to level with me. I have witnesses stating both of you were with the deceased several times and that he was aggravated on at least one of those occasions. A witness stated they heard a screaming match at Mr. Nelson's apartment building. Then I have witnesses that put you at the deceased's car accident, sneaking around. Planting or removing evidence is a federal crime. If there's something you need to tell me, now is your only chance. He's a big guy. Maybe you were just protecting yourself?" He leaned back in the chair, watching me.

I realized he wasn't surprised by my being near the scene earlier. He was just trying to get me to say something to pounce on. "Wait, no, I wasn't doing anything with evidence. Promise!" I dug into my backpack and pulled out the edited clue. "Here, we're all here playing a kind of puzzle treasure hunt, and one of the answers was behind the building, so I had to move it and give out new clues to everything. That's all I was doing!"

"Can I have this? I'll need to check out your story."

"Of course. I'm happy to help in any way I can." I handed him the paper. "I don't know anything about the rest of what you said. We're just here trying to host this event. Whatever was going on with him wasn't with us. And please check with everyone downstairs. I texted them when I had to change the location of the stamp."

His expression didn't change, but he granted me leave to send in the next person.

My legs felt weak as I walked to my room. My brain was full of stories where innocent people went to jail. What if he didn't dig deeper and wanted to go the easy route of pinning it on a stranger? What if the truth really didn't prevail?

Chapter Fifteen

I plopped down in the oversized chair in the corner of my room and contemplated never leaving again. It was a nice, safe chair. No stalkers. No killers. No bugs. I should sell the house and stay as far from this cursed town as possible. Become a beekeeping hermit. I tucked my knees up to my chin, hugging them against me. All the gossip was happening in the living room downstairs, but I was peopled out.

The letterboxers were all fine. Unless one of them did this? Very few were even at the inn when it happened. I shuddered, wondering if the murderer slept under the same roof. But as far as I knew, no one staying with us was local. The victim was a local guy. Maybe this wasn't even a murder. Maybe this was just a rash of bizarre, random events. He could have stumbled out of the hospital, dazed, ended up here, and hit his head on the bench. Perfect. Nice and clean, and no need to stress over. Aliens. It could have been aliens.

I stuffed the dead body trauma securely in denial land and focused on what I did know. Okay, not a murderer, but there was still a strong case that there was a stalker after Trace among them. I needed to figure out who in my group had started letterboxing less than a few months ago. We think the calls began a month ago, but with all the spam and other junk calls, it was hard to pin it down. It wouldn't be someone local as it started back home. So, I needed to remove all old-timers and anyone not from our area of Virginia, Maryland, or the District of Columbia area. Well, that sure narrows it down.

I pulled up the event website and crossed out anyone who had signed up before the first call was placed. Then, looking at their stats, I crossed out everyone who had been letterboxing for longer than the past three months. Not everyone updated their stats online, so this wasn't the most accurate way of verifying identity. However, I had a list to start with. It was something.

I left Nick's name on there, though I wasn't thrilled about it. The others I was left with were Zack, Nathan, Chris, Clara, Sue, Russ, and Ninja Turtle. I didn't know where Nathan called home, but he was staying on the list. I crossed off everyone that came as a family. Granted, this wasn't the most scientific method, but I had to start somewhere. This needed to end.

That didn't account for the names in the rooms and tents who hadn't registered for the event but showed up anyway, like Bob. I still wasn't sure why he was here. I tapped my pen on the paper, thinking. Whoever was doing this would want to be close to her. Now that I had my suspect list, it was time to start paying attention to my guests and find out more information. It was a useful distraction from the dead guy and something I should have done from the start.

I was readying to unwrap from my blanket cocoon and start my murder board when Trace burst in.

"Remi! There was another text." Her hand shook a little as she held out the phone to me. 'Happy spending this time with you!'

"He's here. I know he's here." She sat down in the chair beside me, covered in notes, and assumed my position of arms curled around her knees. What a pair we were.

I stood up, took the blanket, and approached her like I would an injured animal, talking softly. I draped my blanket around her. "Do you know if the Sheriff or any of the police are still downstairs?"

She shook her head. "They left a bit ago."

"Okay, here's what we'll do." My crises may have left me shattered, but give me someone else's, and I could rally in a heartbeat. I knelt beside the chair. "Tonight, you're going to bunk in my room, and tomorrow, we'll get this to the police."

She laid her head down on her knees.

Just to try all things, I dialed the number, but it was still not accepting incoming calls. I texted Karen a brief recap and a screenshot. First thing Monday morning, I would walk Trace to the phone store to get everything switched to a new number.

I sat on the arm of her chair and put my arm around her shoulders. "We've got this. If he's here, he's got to be part of the group of letterboxers. I've narrowed it down to a small list. We can do this."

"You're going to finally live your true life as Nancy Drew," Trace teased, her mood lifting.

"And like her, it'll be with a little help from my friends." I gave her one last shoulder squeeze before getting up to grab my list. "First things first. Who did you spend actual time with today?"

"Ugh. Everyone. We all kept running into each other and chatting. Another big group for lunch. I couldn't tell you who I <u>haven't</u> seen today."

"Okay, not the finest of starts, but no problem. Are you okay on your own in here?"

She nodded.

"Then I'm going to head into the fray downstairs and get as much information as possible. You are in charge of internet sleuthing."

She took a deep breath, and I could see her mentally perking up at having an action she could take.

"Here. My laptop is logged into the letterboxing site. Put in their letterboxing name here and then see what plants and finds they have. Check out social media on them and see if you can find anything. Do they visit cat cafes or work with wildlife rehab. Anything that ties them to you. I'll join the groups, do exchanges, and just listen in or ask a few questions."

"Wait." She put her hand on my arm. "Dude. You found a dead guy today. How are <u>you</u> doing?"

"Compartmentalization is my superpower, remember?" I squeezed her hand for a second. "Later, we can curl up, watch bad movies, and eat junk food while I decompress. Today, I have a job."

Chapter Sixteen

I walked into the living area in time to hear a lady in the back loudly announce, "This next box will be my 1000th find."

No one turned at my arrival, and my brain did a double take seeing a scene of a typical afternoon gathering. People were seated around a small round table and curled up on couches, logbooks and ink pads scattered around.

"Is it weird that he's found so many?" Nick's whisper startled me. "Sorry, didn't mean to scare you. Ready to do an exchange?" He handed me his logbook.

I wanted to tell him that weird didn't even begin to cover how I was feeling. It was surreal knowing there was a dead body just outside the side wall a few hours ago. "That's not the weird part. This is." I gestured to the room of people. "And you," I said, taking his logbook from him.

"I don't mean to be callous, but no one here knew him. It's just words. You and I are the only ones that even saw him," he said.

I inked my personal stamp and stamped it into his book. "Anyway. I stopped counting after 500, but that was about six years ago. Some people love numbers. Some, the art. Whatever floats their boat."

Nick took his logbook back from me and shrugged in agreement. "To me, letterboxing is about following clues and finding the box." He leaned in conspiratorially. "I guess my inner pirate likes to hunt for treasure."

I smiled, visualizing him in a pirate outfit, scouring the forest for Tupperware boxes, a spyglass tucked into his belt. "Some people like to just sit and stamp to collect all the cool images," I said.

"That would be my guy." Clara winked at Chris who was sitting beside her on the couch. Her smile showing deep laugh lines. Sit him in a corner and hand him stamps, and he's happy. Tell him we're going on a ten-mile hike, and there is rebellion." His shirt pictured a gnome in a Sherlock hat.

Find any hobby, and there will be quirks. I put my stuff down and shoved my hands in my front pockets. There was space on the well-worn couch for me, but I stood there awkwardly.

"So, you've been in here awhile?" I asked Clara. I paused, trying to figure out how to ask what I wanted to know. "Has anyone been talking about what happened?" The straightforward approach seemed best.

"They were for a bit," Chris admitted. "But all we've had to deal with is to answer some questions about it, and things gradually faded back to letterboxing talk.

"Huh. So, you two have been doing this for a while then? For some reason, I thought you were new to the hobby." I said. Clara and Chris were on my list, but they didn't sound like newbies.

"Oh, we've been doing this for years. The only thing we're new at is each other." Clara said, smiling at Chris. "We met while letterboxing, got married, and I moved out this way to be with him. I'm so glad you had this event. It's a perfect way for me to meet the local group."

"We had no idea Trace did this too. I've been having tea at the Cozy Cat for a couple of months now and, I never would have guessed." Chris said.

I froze. "You go to the cat cafe pretty regularly?" I asked.

He looked down at his logbook. "We lost our cat this year. I go there and read on my lunch break."

Clara laid her hand on Chris's arm. "He almost adopted one of them, but found out someone had beat him to the adoption." She said.

He took a deep breath and started cleaning up his stamps and ink. "It was probably for the best. I'm going to head out and try these clues." He said, holding up some random papers.

I had been about to mentally cross them both off my list but decided to have them stay. Neither struck me as a stalker, but would I know one if I met them? Did Chris blame Trace for losing out on the adoption? Or has a secret crush. He wouldn't share that with Clara. That would wipe out my basis of checking on the letterboxing side of things, so I opted to stay with my original plan. Where was my next victim? I spied Ninja Turtle tucked into a corner table alone, half-hidden behind a large plant.

I walked over and pointed at the image on his logbook. "Cute turtle stamp. I don't remember seeing it in any of the boxes around the area," I said.

He covered it with his hand, giving a half-shrug. "I just started, and I've probably only been places after you've gone. And I don't tend to log boxes in online. Computers and I have a love-hate relationship," he said.

You, Mr. Ninja Turtle, are now at the top of the list. "So, where-abouts are you from?"

"Oh, uh, just a few hours north." He hedged.

Before I could find a way to narrow that answer down, he looked over my shoulder and asked, "Do you want to try for my personal stamp?"

His lack of eye contact was disconcerting. I glanced back and saw Nick there with a confused expression. Why was he everywhere I went? For his benefit, I explained, "A personal stamp is a separate stamp you carry with you, and the person has to answer a question or do an action to get it. For Capt'n Nemo over there, you have to sing a sea shanty."

Turning back to Ninja Turtle I asked, "Sure, what do we need to do?"

"I'd only found out about it here, so the carve isn't great, but the clue is easy. Tell me which Teenage Mutant Ninja Turtle wore the orange mask."

"Donatello?" Nick offered.

"Kowabunga!" He handed us a stamp of all four turtle heads grouped together.

While Nick took his turn stamping, I decided to try again. "I'm about two hours away, too. By Sterling?" I waited, hoping he would now jump in with his location.

He nodded as he gathered up his materials. "Alright, see you on the trials." He brushed by Trace coming into the room and skittered to the side, his head down.

"Well, that wasn't awkward at all," she said, joining us.

"He's setting off my spidey senses," I said. "He stays on the list."

"You two listing men?" Nick asked, doing a comic eyebrow wriggle.

I looked at Trace, who gave me a 'you get to adlib this one' shrug.

"No, we're trying to find people new to the hobby. So. We. Can maybe get them more involved or something?" I was shaking my head a little. Lying was not my forte.

April came through the door from the kitchen and saved me from myself. "I need to grab these two for a moment." She took hold of our elbows and steered us into the kitchen.

"Looks like someone is in trouble," Nick said.

Oh my god. His eyes twinkle when he smiles. I didn't have time for this. Maybe I'm having a weird reaction from shock.

Once through the door, Alice turned and gave me a huge hug. "First, are you okay?"

I found myself almost tearing up at the concern, but my brain focused on the fact that a Second was coming. The second in a list is rarely good news.

"Look, hon, I don't want you to worry or get upset." She said. Too late for that.

"The police want to talk to you again. They couldn't get through on your phone, so they called our main line and asked you to come in for more questions."

"Okay, I'm sure that's normal," I said, not believing it.

"There's more."

"Spill it, Alice. I can take it." I steeled myself.

"I've got a friend in the Sheriff's station, and there's been an anonymous call to check on the various unpleasant things that tend to happen to people who bother Trace. Did something happen back home? They're checking into something there."

Chapter Seventeen

I could hear the pounding of my heart. I couldn't breathe. Someone guided me down into a hard wooden chair.

"Who would say something like that?" As soon as I said it, I knew. The same person we've been trying to track down. Trace's stalker was giving the police, me, wrapped in a bow, for the things they've done. That means whoever is doing that is the same person who murdered two people.

I looked up into Trace's eyes and knew she'd come to the same conclusion.

"We've gotta get you outta here," I said.

Alice knelt beside me. "Maybe not. Here, the police are investigating, and we can work together to see that she stays in a group.

Besides, it sounds like the people who bother her are in danger for now."

"Okay." I nodded. "That makes sense. But we need to figure this out." I turned to Trace. "You know I always lose at Clue. Tell me you found something."

"Maybe. That's what I came down to tell you. Someone named the Fisherman just started posting finds today. Have you met him?"

"Now he's letterboxing? Seriously, what is his deal?"

Trace looked at me, and I realized I hadn't clued her in.

"The Fisherman is Nathan. Tent Nathan. With the fisherman's vest." I said.

"So one minute, he's hiking the Appalachian Trail. He happens to camp where we head to, and now he's part of the group event we're running."

"Definitely someone to keep an eye on. You should check in with the Sheriff's office to see if they talked with him. And Ninja Turtle was acting pretty squirrely. Oh! And who knew Scott was bugging you?" I asked.

"Anyone out in the groups yesterday. Scott wasn't being rude, but he, um, was definitely showing interest. I've tried getting ahold of the police for updates, but the are swamped with the festival in town. My tests don't rate manpower right now."

"Dangit. I hoped it would just be from the diner, and we could see who Jake remembered."

Trace checked in with the police as she walked outside with me. I needed air and movement. I spent a few moments looking around at the ever-growing group of people. I veered to avoid the part of the yard that led to the garden. That wasn't something I wanted to relive anytime soon. No one had seemed to have a robust interest in Trace. But would a stalker be obvious? Or shy in person preferring to fantasize from afar? Worse case, I was keeping Trace with me as much as I could.

Trace sighed as she got off the phone. "He was out, but I left a message with the deputy with our cell numbers. I also mentioned our theory of the stalker turning the story against us."

"Well, it looks like Nathan's done a disappearing act. I don't even see his tent. In ISpy games, you can sometimes get hints. I would gladly buy a hint at this point.

"We should check and see if Nathan is hanging out back at yours." She said.

Yours, she said. My house. Even after a day of shock, that phrase made my heart warm.

"Let's take the cut-through path this time."

Before we reached the tree line, we spied a group with Zack, Nick, Bob, Sue, and Jake. Jake? And again with Bob. He'd never shown the slightest interest in my hobbies before. Why was he here? Bob has never done a thing in his life without an ulterior motive. I stopped dead. Could it be him? Was this about trying to scare Trace off to get me back now that I have something he could get his hands on? He'd tried unsuccessfully to come between us before, but would he go this far? Maybe he got himself in too deep on something. I needed to figure out what his angle was for being here.

Jake waved us over to join them. I noticed Sue had abandoned her perfectly ironed clothes for a t-shirt, jeans, and a messy ponytail. Nick left when we walked up, mumbling about having somewhere to be.

"Guess the honeymoon is over," Bob remarked.

I frowned at him but refused to take the bait. I'd figure out what, if anything, was wrong with Nick later.

"Hey," Jake said, looking at me. "Um, I hope you don't mind me dropping by."

"Of course not. How'd you even know where to find us?" I asked.

"Small town, remember?" He smiled and ran his hand through his short, dark hair. "Look, I wondered if you'd be looking for extra hands to work on your place? I do construction part-time, and I'd, um, love to come by and help."

Bob's bark of a "No" and Trace's "Yes" were instantaneous.

He looked a little hurt by Bob's outburst.

"That would actually be a great help," I said. "There's a ton of cleanup we need to do starting next week."

"I could start today if you wanted me to."

"Small town gossip must have failed you." I teased. "The house is tented for a few days, getting rid of pests. It's too dangerous to go in until they give everything clear. But come Tuesday, please swing by."

He smiled and tipped an imaginary hat. "Yes, ma'am."

Trace moved closer to me once he'd left. "He likes you," she said in teasing voice.

I appreciated her attempt to get my mind off of reality. "Don't be ridiculous. And we are not talking about this." Out of the corner of my eye, I could see the tension in Bob's mouth, a sure sign he was grinding his teeth. Sue and Zack had stayed quiet. "You two enjoying yourself?" I asked.

Zack nodded. "Great fun. Jake was telling us all about the house you inherited. Your Aunt sounds like she'd have some great stories to tell. Are you going to move out here?"

Trace's shoulder bumped me. "Yup. When we finish it, this will be the premiere board game cafe and Bed and Breakfast on the East Coast."

"You're moving too?" Sue asked.

I gave Trace a one-handed hug. "We've had this as a dream plan for years." I looked over to where Nick was sitting on a low stone wall. "Hey, I'm going to go check on Nick. Can you hang here a sec? In the group." I stressed. "Then we'll go do that thing?" I didn't want to give any more fodder to the rumor mill.

I'd probably owe her a slice of cheesecake for leaving her with Bob. Nick hadn't gone too far away. His back was to the group, so I walked to stand in front of him, keeping Trace in sight.

He looked up at me without smiling. "What can I do for you?"

No sparkle in the eyes now. "You can tell me why I'm suddenly getting the cold shoulder."

"I don't like games. Your boyfriend over there filled me in quite a bit on you. And then made it perfectly clear that he didn't appreciate my being around so much. He's got quite a jealousy issue."

"Whoa, there. Let's back up about three of four false statements and listen. I do not have a boyfriend. That walking, speaking pseudo-human you just spoke to is my ex-boyfriend of almost six months, who I left after he stole my life savings for a get-rich-quick scheme. I don't play games unless it's the kind with meeples, no one tells me what to do, and quite frankly, I'm not too thrilled you immediately thought the worst of me without checking first. What is this, some sort of male code to warn others off their property? Well, you can take that attitude and shove it."

By then, I had worked myself up into quite a head of steam and I stomped away. I didn't wait for a response.

"Excuse me, can I have this?" I grabbed a soda from someone I passed and liberally poured it over Bob. "Tell Sean it's too dangerous here, and you need to go home."

"But..." he started.

I got up close to his face. "Now."

Chapter Eighteen

Trace kept pace with me as I stomped down the path. I'd calmed down by the time I got to the overgrown hedge separating the two properties. Pushing my way through the hedge onto my land was like opening the doors to Narnia. The last thing I could call my own land was a postage-sized townhouse lawn I could mow with a weedwhacker. I stopped for a moment to take in the back of the castle. Even covered in white tenting and "Warning, Do Not Enter" signs, seeing it was enough to cool my anger down.

"Soon," I said to myself.

Trace nudged me and pointed towards the woods. "I don't see his tent."

"Let's walk the tree line around and see if anything comes up." I pulled a small bag out of my backpack to pick up the trash I saw earlier. I had little faith he'd gone back to clean up. Looking toward Alice's, I spied a glint from the roof and waved in case Jason was looking our way. I was about to text him to see if he saw Nathan but realized he wouldn't know who that was. Asking him if he saw a blue tent would be equally useless with the current state of their yard.

Nathan's abandoned campsite didn't offer anything other than some fast-food wrappers. There were the remains of an attempt at a fire, but he hadn't dug any fire pit, so we're lucky he failed at starting it. We'd had rain lately, but having an uncontrolled fire was never a good idea. One thing I knew about him now was that he was not a seasoned camper, and I doubted he was here for trail hiking or letterboxing.

I picked up the candy wrappers and tried to erase evidence of the fire. The last thing I needed was another hiker, thinking this was the place to stop.

"Was someone meant to be here today?" Trace asked.

I looked where she was facing and saw a middle-aged woman in a business suit striding towards us, a clipboard clutched in her arm.

"No way," I said, recognizing her as she got closer. "Mary?" Unlike at the diner, she presented a polished, official look. Her expression was just as contentious.

"Ms. McKenna," she greeted me but ignored my outstretched hand. She looked down at the papers on her clipboard as if surprised by what she found. "I see you have applied to turn this structure into a BnB."

She nodded and rifled through the papers. "Well, as you know, we need to make sure that is best for our small town and there is already a building next door that will be an Inn."

She looked at me and smiled coldly. "I'm not sure I can support this request with the council."

"I understand your concern, but we will be offering two entirely different experiences. I'm sure once I can talk to the council, they'll feel that it's a worthwhile business." I said, my mind reeling. Why did no one mention my arch nemesis was also someone who could decide my fate?

Mary clucked her tongue. "And you wish to have a permit to serve food?" She made some more marks on the page.

"When is the next council meeting?" Trace asked moving to stand beside me in support.

"Next week Tuesday. I'm not sure we have enough time on the schedule to allow for speakers. You can try contacting the office to see if they fit you in." She turned and walked away from us. Before she got around the corner, she turned back. "Oh, of course. How could I forget? The council secretary is out until Monday." She smirked and left.

"I don't think she'll invite me over for the holidays," I said trying to sound unconcerned.

Going back to Trace's room, I flopped down on her bed. "What a flippen day," I said.

She paced around the room nervously. "Something feels wrong. Have you ever walked into a place and felt like someone has moved things, but everything seems okay?"

"More different than Alice cleaning it this afternoon?" I asked, raising up on my elbows.

"Huh, maybe that's all it is. Maybe I'm just getting paranoid." She shook her head. "Here, see my ducks." Her ducks said 'rural' and 'oil.' So far, I haven't seen a connection, but I wasn't at my best. I jotted down the words with the others.

Trace rubbed her shoulders with her hands, stopped, felt the front of her neck, and went to the bathroom. I heard her scamper around for a moment.

"It's gone." She moved a few more items around. "My necklace is gone."

I called Alice from the room phone and asked her to come up. Trace was methodically taking everything off the shelves one at a time to look around in any possible hidey hole.

"Alice, did you clean the rooms today?" I asked

"Yes, is something wrong?" She looked around the room, trying to see what was out of order.

"Trace had left her necklace in the bathroom but can't find it. I thought maybe it would be in the bag if you vacuumed it?"

"I just swept in here with the hardwood floors, and there was nothing but dust bunnies." Alice touched Trace's arm. "Hon, have you checked under the dresser? When stuff falls, it bounces on these floors, and they end up in the oddest places. Jason swears we have gremlins."

We all started searching the room, inside the vents, anywhere a necklace might have fallen to become lodged. The expression on Trace's face made my heart hurt.

"We will find it," I promised her. Maybe you put it in a pocket out of habit, and then it fell on the trail. But even if I have to buy metal detectors for everyone to go over every inch of ground, we will find it." I meant every word, and she nodded, but I could tell the loss was eating at her. It was the only thing she had left of the parents she lost at eighteen.

Maybe this place was cursed.

Chapter Nineteen

Having Nick at my bedroom door would have been more enticing before our fight. Also, Trace would be over soon. He leaned on the doorframe, not meeting my eyes.

"You lost your clue packet?" My tone was a bit frostier than before.

"Hey, I'm sorry to bother you. I can't figure out where I would have left it." Nick ran his fingers through his hair. A small part stayed sticking straight up, and I resisted the urge to pat it back down for him. I almost regretted packing my old threadbare, comfy robe versus the satiny one.

I turned to look out the window and back at him. "This couldn't wait until daylight?" The clue packets were five feet away. I could walk over, grab one and close the door in seconds. But he had made me as grouchy as a wet cat.

"Well, yes." He looked down at his shoes for a moment and then up at me. "I mainly wanted to apologize. You were right. I should have just talked to you."

As he was on my suspect list, I begrudgingly admitted to myself I couldn't blame him for thinking I could have done something, too. For all he knew, I was a killer. He literally found me over a dead body. We didn't know each other. "It's okay. But next time you want to know something, ask me directly."

He smiled. "Deal."

"Alright, let's do this thing." I stepped back and waved him into my bedroom. The packets were on the other side of the bed.

"That's a little fast for me." He smiled.

I tilted my head, confused, and even my brain caught up with the awkward position I'd managed to get myself into. I looked from the bed to him. "No, no, no," I said it a few times in case I was unclear. "Meaning, let's grab you a clue packet together for you. They're on the desk."

I wrapped my arms around myself and stood away from the bed and the entrance, giving him plenty of room to get past me and to the desk.

"I'd talked to Trace earlier and she told me about your boardgame place. That sounds fun. I haven't played one in ages." Nick said

"Well, we're going to have to fix that." I replied, already mulling over a good game to start him with. First, I needed to dig for information. "Was it the cat café you'd met Trace at before here?"

I hadn't heard any such thing, but this undercover spy stuff was new to me.

He stopped for a second. "No, I met you both here." He tilted his head, seeming a little confused by my line of question, but didn't pursue it. "Thanks for the clues. Sorry again, and maybe we can hike tomorrow?"

His smile faded a bit when I took too long to respond. I wanted to, but my brain was hurting. Or it was low blood sugar, and I needed a donut.

"Let's go with maybe. I'm pretty swamped." I gestured randomly to the clue packets. "Hey, are you doing okay. I mean, how did your interview with the Sheriff go?"

"Pretty quick. I didn't know Scott. There wasn't anything I could give them to help. He mainly wanted to know how much time I'd spent with you during the day." He held up his clue packet. "So, yeah, you know how to find me."

I smiled as I saw him out the door, glad our tension was resolving. Nice, polite and noncommittal. I didn't commit to it, but I didn't blow him off. There wasn't really time. I had a council out for blood, a stalker to find, and apparently, my name to clear. Lost in thought, I found my hand was still on the door when it vibrated from someone banging on it. 'I am popular tonight.'

This visitor was far less welcome. "Bob," I said with zero inflection.

"WHO is this guy you keep spending time with?"

"Not you. Other than that, it's none of your business." I kept my voice calm and without any tone. "What part of 'Go Home' did you not understand?"

I closed the door on him, admiring myself for not slamming it in his face. What was the creep doing - spying up at my room from his tent? I went over to the window with views of the tents and closed the blinds and curtains. He shouldn't even be able to get a silhouette now.

After a few moments, Trace walked in and threw herself length-wise on the bed. "It was Professor Plum in the Study with the Wrench," she said. She glanced at me when I didn't respond. "Oooh, from that look, you either made a faux pas, or Bob bothered you."

"Let's go with option C or both! Nick came to my room for clues, and I behaved like a hormonal teenager. I have zero game."

"No games. It's been a long time since you were single. Take it slow, and the right guy will be fine with things."

I tossed a pillow at her as I knew she was right.

"Do I want to know what Bob did?" She asked, hugging the pillow.

I shook my head. "Nothing worthwhile, just being Bob."

Trace's phone rang, and she jumped a little in her skin.

"Trace, you're going to have a panic attack if you keep jumping every time your phone beeps. I looked down; it was just an automatic county flash flood warning. Nothing that affected us in this part of the county.

"Here, give me your phone." I grabbed mine from the desk. "You take mine. If that guy calls again, maybe I can get something out of him."

She seemed relieved to be rid of the thing. "To be honest, if it wasn't for safety reasons, I would just leave the thing in the room, but I don't like being out on the trails without some way to communicate."

"Oooh. Does this mean I can play your games?" I smiled, pretending to scroll through her icons, knowing her rabid need to have high scores on her favorites.

"Touch my word game score, and I'll post as you on your Facebook page. I'm sure I can think of something to say that you've always wanted to share."

"Touche. Your scores are safe with me." I tucked her phone in my robe pocket, pleased to see her smiling and less jumpy. I wished the jerk would call. I had a few choice things to say to him about his manner of courting. The Sheriff recommended getting a new number as the first deterrent if blocking the call didn't work. It was going to tick Trace off to do it. For now, she was going to be bunking with me. "Come on, you should stay here tonight. Let's throw on a bad movie. It'll be like a slumber party."

"This is ridiculous. I'm an adult, and it's late. I'm not watching a movie. I need to get to sleep, and I can do that in my room."

"I'm sure you are quite capable of that. Now, which side of the bed do you want?" The thing was a king, so we could both sleep comfortably.

She groaned, realized she'd lost, and curled up on the left side of the bed. While she scrolled through the available channels, I peeked out the window, surprised to see quite a bit of activity. I'm not sure I'd want to go out night boxing with a crime scene tape still scattered around the lawn. Night 'boxing was basically the same as during the day, but you follow reflector light trails through the woods or just use a flashlight. The boxes were all on a reasonably flat loop trail to cut down on the possibility of anyone twisting an ankle. At least folks were heading off into groups with plenty of flashlights. It was going to take more than one body to stop them.

Chapter Twenty

I woke up to the click of a door shutting and the sound of someone running down the hallway. The TV was now playing an alien invasion, and Trace was fast asleep. I hadn't even made it through our movie. I got out of bed, now wide awake, and opened the door to peek out. The hallway was empty, and I didn't hear anything from the stairs. Horror movie rules said I should investigate on my own, but I went the cautious route. I locked the door and jammed a walking pole in place to keep it shut. For all I knew, the sounds may have been from the TV or another part of the farmhouse. It's old, sound travels, and I was disoriented from sleep. My racing heart told me it wasn't the TV. There was no way I'd get back to sleep now.

Instead, I grabbed Trace's phone and started googling everything I could on stalkers and crime reports. Had I made myself the next target? I didn't find news on people being reported around Trace's apartment, but that wasn't a surprise. As far as I knew, stalkers didn't generally go after more than one person at a time. The crime rate in Trace's zip code was meager, and there was no news on the guy that died in the apartment. Something was fishy with that, and it wasn't fermented herring.

Usually, I needed more than six hours of sleep to function. This was not my night. After trying soothing podcasts, I gave up and just read until it was a decent enough hour to go downstairs to enjoy a quiet cup of hot tea and a muffin. I locked the door behind me and double-checked it before I left.

Nick was on the couch in the main sitting room, leaning down to the left with both hands moving. Looking over his shoulder to see what he was doing, I found a large, brownish-red, and white mound of fur almost as high as the armrest with a furry head tilted up in adoration. Baron, my Australian Shepherd, was enjoying a thorough head scratch, his eyes staring at Nick in adoration.

Baron? What was Baron doing here? My feet stopped as thoughts clicked into place. Bob had taken Baron, making it quite clear that I didn't have time to properly care for a dog on my own, and after all, it was his money that paid for the puppy, so why should I get him? Why? Because Bob was a soulless monster who didn't like dogs. Not that he would ever harm one. He just preferred to hire out the care of a dog to others. He was the same kind of person who would send their offspring to boarding school at the youngest age they could. Baron was a photo op to him. I softly called his name to make sure Baron didn't have a twin. He came over and smushed his nose into my arm in greeting.

"How did you get here, boy?" I asked, automatically checking him out for problems while giving him some big hug squishes. I had missed him more than I ever missed Bob.

Nick walked over and handed me a folded note. "A lady opened the door and dropped him off about fifteen minutes ago. I was relaxing while everyone was sleeping, and he's been keeping me company. I hope I wasn't supposed to come get you as soon as he showed up."

Baron's butt wiggled in agreement. Now, there were two people to pet him. What could be better than this? I opened the note, skimmed the short missive, and crumpled it into a tiny ball. What was Bob playing at? First, he shows up with my tent after never showing the slightest interest in camping while we were together, and now he has returned my dog while I'm staying at an inn hours from home.

"I didn't even know he was coming. Sorry about all that fur." I motioned to the now fur-encrusted jeans he was wearing. It was time to get this boy into a grooming appointment.

"I don't mind." He gave Baron another scratch on the head. "My uncle always had dogs around. So I enjoy being around them. Though those little dogs creep me out a bit. Oh, there's the spot, eh boy?" He asked as Baron pressed his head against him.

While Nick continued to shower Baron with attention, I took a few deep breaths to clear my head, which was hard to do with Nick so close to my leg. Baron hadn't left me since coming over to say hi. I didn't know what game Bob was playing, but I wasn't signing up.

I looked up when Alice came in and motioned to Baron. "Alice, I'm so sorry about this."

"Oh, my word, he's beautiful!" She came over. "Is it okay for me to pet him?"

"He would mope if you didn't." He calmly sat there as she oohed and aah-ed over his thick, soft fur.

"My ex dropped him off for reasons known only to him. If you could tell me the name of a kennel in town, I'll get him out of here right away."

"Oh, please. To be honest, we aren't going to allow pets here when we open, just because of the upkeep issues, but I love having dogs around. If you can vouch for his behavior, Baron can stay the weekend." She leaned in and whispered, "You could always bring him as far as I'm concerned."

I almost laughed when Baron turned his nose towards me as if saying, 'Please, Mom, please?'

"You rock, Alice. He won't be any trouble, and I'll, uh, help vacuum," I said, looking down at the fur covering her brown pants.

I gathered Baron's leash and went outside to 'thank' Bob. If he wasn't careful, I would thank him with a stick. Then Sheriff Marrow would have a reason to think I was capable of violence, so bad idea. I'd been fighting to get Baron back from him for months, and now he has decided to drop him off?

Bob's tent was empty, and I didn't see him in the scattered groups setting up for the day.

"He took Sean into town for breakfast," Sue said, walking up to me.

"Thanks. Well, a walk into town would give us the exercise we both need." I said. Besides, driving the curving roads didn't take much more time than the straight back route through the property, and my car was still blocked in.

"Mind if I come along? I'm a little weirded out still by yesterday and could use the company." She settled her backpack into place.

"Not if you don't mind frequent stops while Baron learns all the new smells. But be warned, when I see Bob, I'll need some alone time."

She smiled wistfully. "He talks about you all the time. You're lucky to have such a supportive boyfriend."

I shook my head. "He is NOT my boyfriend. He's just insanely good at manipulating people into thinking that." I paused and decided to be nosey. "How long have you and Russ been together?" I asked.

She grimaced. "Never. We just carpooled here."

While walking, I sent a quick text to Trace, letting her know to keep my phone and to have two other people with her today if possible. I hoped we were overreacting to this caller of Trace's, but part of me wanted to hire an armed bodyguard to follow her around twenty-four seven until we were sure.

I spied Bob on the edge of town. "This is where we need to break up. Have a great time out there." I told Sue before channeling all my rising frustration into stomping over to deal with him.

"Morning," he greeted me. "Kind of early for you, isn't it? What is Baron doing here? Hoping to have us all back together as a family for the weekend?" He smiled.

I looked around and saw Sean heading into a bakery with a pink-striped awning. Pots of flowers on the outside surrounded a chalkboard of today's goodies. A drawing of a steaming coffee cup reminded me I'd need caffeine soon.

"Don't play with me, Bob. You dropped him off hoping to get me kicked out of the inn."

"Well, I won't lie. Having your company in the tent would be nice, but I haven't left the area since we got here. Sean and I went out for pizza last night with a few other boxers. Ask Chris, Clara, or Zack. Sean and I were in the tent after that until this morning."

"Nick said a lady dropped him off with your note stating, "Please watch Baron for me, sweetheart."

He had the good grace to look mildly embarrassed. "That was the note I left with my...friend so she'd watch him while we were here."

Suddenly, it all became crystal clear. Bob abandoned the dog with a current girlfriend to give him time to come here and hope to win me back on the side. He did love to keep all options open.

"I can't believe you left him somewhere without checking if it was okay!" My hissing was whispered as letterboxers and town people were walking near us. I did not need a huge scene on the first official day. "Baron is going home with me."

Sean came out holding a muffin the size of his hand, and we both tried to cover the heated argument. He was a smart kid and wasn't fooled. "Want me to take Baron for a walk while you guys talk?"

"We. Are. Done." I emphasized the 'done' staring at Bob. "Uncle Bob said that Baron should live with me after the 'boxing event.'"

I turned to Sean. "You know you're always welcome to come visit him."

There was no way Bob would continue a petty argument in front of Sean, so he pursed his lips together and nodded, acknowledging defeat.

"Great!" He bit into the muffin and started towards downtown Main Street.

"Let me at least buy you a coffee." He'd slipped into his charming suit. "I just want a chance to talk with you. What we had was too good to let go."

I shook my head. "Bob, we didn't 'let it go'. It disintegrated slowly, lie after lie."

Chapter Twenty-One

"You know, you're the only one I care about. I can be better." Bob's eyes pleaded with me, and deep in my heart, there was a tiny flicker of temptation.

But I doused the traitorous feeling quickly. "Let this go. No more calls. Emails. Nothing." I shook my head, exhausted from dealing with this. I took a deep breath and walked away from him straight to the bakery.

Baron did a "sit and stay" at the side of the door. Once through the doorway, I took a few moments to calm myself. Each time, walking away from Bob was a little easier. I looked out the window to see Sue consoling Bob, her hand on his arm. He was lapping up the attention. I was torn between warning her away and feeling relieved that he may have found someone else to bother. If things kept up, I'd at least have to mention it to her.

The bakery was the first stop for some letterboxers, with how I adjusted the starting points. I couldn't promise them any sales out of it, but the owner seemed to enjoy the spirit of the game.

The front of the store had morphed from chocolate-covered strawberries and fudge to UFO-themed cookies. There line was five people deep with more coming in behind me, but the cashier was getting them in and out quickly. I waited my turn after grabbing a chocolate-shaped alien for myself.

I caught the shopkeeper before he ran to get more stock. "Hi, I just wanted to check in and see if leaving the candy bars here would still be okay?"

"Yes, yes, not a problem. We don't need to do anything except hand out the candy bars to anyone who says the clue, right?"

I nodded.

"As long as they don't mind waiting their turn if I have customers. Can you believe all this craziness over some lights?" He asked speaking lowly.

"It's not what I was expecting. Has it ever been like this before?"

"No, and we've had reports of strange lights for years. Something about this one set things off. Sorry to rush you, but I must I have put another batch of aliens in to chill. You might want to check in with the bookstore. They ended up having some special signings today."

I handed him the packet of personalized wrapped candy bars, which would only be given to people asking for the Rubber Duck special. Inside was a clue: *Chocolate is toxic to alien rubber ducks. Now that you know what defeats the ducks, you should read up on the best place to trap them when they come to town, or if you have a blue sticker on your clues, you should check out the museum. There have been rumors that this is not the first duck invasion to strike this town. The museum may know how they survived.*

That would make their next stop the bookstore or the museum, depending on which track they were taking. Taking the advice, I decided to check in with the bookstore to confirm they were still on board as well.

Baron and I avoided Bob and Sue by skittering around the corner onto Main Street. And stopped. The quaint, historic town was gone. In its place was a food truck-laden, vendor-stall mecca of commerce. But not the trade of handcrafted artisan wares. These were stalls sporting green alien balloons, phaser guns, t-shirts, and assorted items I wasn't sure I wanted to know about. People were holding up signs of 'Welcome Visitors' and 'Take Me With You,' but also a smattering of 'This is the End '-type dire warnings.

"Well, this looks different," I said. Baron wagged his butt in agreement. I'm sure his brain was focused on how many people would try to pet him.

A man approached me wearing an old-fashioned, ill-fitting brown suit. His suit vest was covered with space patches. His beard grayed and almost scraggly enough to be called unkempt. He shoved a clipboard towards me. "Sign the petition."

It came across as a statement instead of a request. He held a pen out to me, shaking it slightly when I didn't grab it.

"What is it for?" I asked.

"To have a mandatory lights out at 8 p.m. tonight throughout the county." He shook the pen at me again.

I took it and the clipboard hoping the paper on it would have something explaining the request. No luck. My eyebrows raised, I waited, hoping he would elaborate. "Why would we want to do that?"

"'Cause you need to have all the blasted man-made lights off so you can see if there are any visitors. If they're too far into the mountains or woods, we need all the extra visibility we can get."

The look of disgust was so blatant I almost scolded myself for asking such an obvious question. "Look, Mr..."

"Charlie."

"I'm not a resident here, so my signature wouldn't count anyway." I handed the clipboard and pen back to him.

"Your gettin' that stone house up on the hill, ain't ya? Then you count." He pushed the clipboard back to me.

It's like my inheritance was on a billboard somewhere. Small town living was going to be an adjustment. He won points by asking to pet Baron. To appease him, I scribbled my name and handed it back. This was not a battle I cared enough to fight. "I know there were some reports of a few weird lights, but is this a normal turnout for the yearly UFO festival?" I motioned around at the shopping center around us, hoping he'd talk more.

"Nah. That online guy. What's his name? You know that fella that has the best of lists? He mentioned our town as the best place to see a UFO in the U.S. and then mentioned the meteor shower we're due for, starting tonight. 'Bout then, the hotels booked up in a few hours, and these crazies appeared."

He looked towards the stalls and crowds and back to me. "But they won't see anything. They don't know the best spots. Watch out for yourself." He tipped his head to me and walked on.

Trace came up beside me and gave me a one-armed hug. "Boy, when you plan a themed event, you go all out!" She teased.

"Ugggh. This turnout will make things a little more difficult, but it does work, I guess." She was wearing a T-shirt that said Beam Me Up.

She noticed me check out the shirt. "Don't be jealous. I got you one, too." She handed me a small bag with a shirt. "Am I supposed to ignore that I left you without a dog this morning, and now you have a dog?" She knelt and gave Baron a good head rub. "Did aliens bring you on a spaceship, Baron? Hmmm?"

She looked up at me. "Come to think of it - you don't have to explain. It's Bob's doing, so why should it ever make sense? I'm happy to see you two back together."

Baron sniffed around at Trace's pockets and sat back seeming disappointed. Usually, when he saw Trace, she had liver treats for him. "Sorry, sweetie, I'll be sure to stock up now that you're here."

"I thought you were staying at the inn this morning and staying with a group?" That seemed safer than screaming at her that her phone call person was unhinged and she shouldn't be alone.

"People sent pics of the town to you, and I had to come see for myself. Don't worry. I walked down with Russ and a bunch of others keeping with the buddy system"

Baron bumped his nose in my arm for attention and gave me an idea. "Do you mind taking him for a bit? I need to check in with the shops and confirm they can still keep the clues on site. They may have decided it's more than they can handle." My ulterior motive being she'd now have a dog keeping an eye on her. No one needed to know he was the gentlest pup on the planet.

I made my way to the bookstore, weaving through the throng of shoppers and people telling me that The Truth was Out There. The baker guy wasn't kidding. I noticed a steady stream of traffic going into the bookstore. I grabbed a napkin off a food cart to wipe the last of the gooey chocolate alien from my hands and wandered over to check out the attraction. The entire front display featured alien and UFO books. Cardboard cutouts in the shape of flying saucers hung from the ceiling. I wondered if he'd let one go after the craze. They would make excellent Halloween decorations.

Sitting at a table with a line streaming from it was an older man with dirty blonde hair and glasses. Book piles covered the table except for the small area he was using to sign books. According to the display, this was the infamous Rudy Ambletree, resident UFO expert and new novelist. His book, They're Here, was propped up, and a full-size poster display sat next to him.

Curious, I waded in and picked up a copy of the book. Instead of being the alien probe horror story of an abduction as I feared it would be, it was a novel. Books are impossible to resist. I went behind one of the taller shelf units and began to read it.

Ten minutes later, I stopped hiding and went to buy the book. The author had a way with words, and the plot was quirky and drama-filled. I wanted to delve into the entire world and see what became of everyone. I flagged down the owner.

"Before I head out, I wanted to confirm these postcards were still okay with you."

"Anything that brings business into the store is good for me."

"Well, I can't promise they'll buy anything..."

He waved my objections away. "If they're book people, I'm sure they'll pick up something." He looked at the book in my hand. "It's just how readers roll. Quite a few people were coming by for your postcards. The crowds don't seem to bother them all. I did move the rack over to the side so it's away from the line."

He walked me over to the register. "One fella did go look at them funny after the one group came in. It was kind of fun watching him try to figure out what was so special about your card. He tried to buy one, but I told him they weren't for sale, so he took a picture with his phone." He stopped and looked over at me. "Hope that's not a problem."

I shook my head. While he rang me up, I did a quick count of the cards left. "No, this card is nothing special for anyone but people in my group."

"If he shows up, you'll know him. No way you can miss Ole' Charlie."

"Wait, is that the same Charlie trying to get everyone to sign a blackout petition?" I asked.

He laughed. "Yup, like I said. You can't miss him. A bit of a believer in the whole government conspiracy to keep us in the dark about alien life on our planet." He waved it away. "But he's harmless. I should warn you about the other Charlie, though. He goes by Chuck, and tends to be a bit more aggressive. He's never hurt anyone but can come across as scary if you're not used to him."

"You have two Charlies in the same town, and they're both Alien guys?" I asked.

"It did cut down on the use of the name for babies, I must admit." he joked, handing me my receipt.

I went to the postcard rack and filled one slot with a postcard from the county bank. On the back of each was a note to get the stamp from the person at the counter and a label with just three numbers. From there, they had to go to the bank and use the code to 'break' into the safe. Inside would be the stamp and their next clue.

The bookstore and bakery were the only two stops that were close to all the action. I mentally crossed my fingers hoping the event would be smooth, even with the unexpected volume of attendees for the space festival.

Leaving the store I saw someone I thought I recognized walking down the road, a cardboard sign held high. I watched and waited to see if she would turn around, and when she did, I couldn't believe it. Clara was carrying a sign that said, '*The ducks are on the way. Prepare yourself.*'

"Ma'am, do you know anything about that individual?"

"Chris?" I cautiously asked the man standing before me, wearing a dark suit and sunglasses. I saw a small, curly cue wire running from his ear down his collar.

"Agent Gamer Geek, ma'am."

"What are you doing?" I dropped my voice to a whisper. "What is she doing?"

"Ma'am, that's classified. Take my card and contact us if you see anything suspicious."

He adjusted his glasses and took his partner's elbow, decked out in a black suit and glasses. They melted into the crowd.

The business card he gave me had an alien on one side, and on the back, it said: *Landing. We've come to Earth for your pizza. Check the third flowerpot at Joe's Pizzeria.*

I laughed, finally catching on that it was a letterboxing clue.

Trace broke through the crowd again with Baron, who was wagging his tail as if she'd just given him alien cupcakes. "Hey, Chris and Clara are too cute. Did you see them? When they came to town, they popped into the thrift store to suit up and have been going through the crowd as Men in Black types. They must have already planned on putting an alien clue in town and had the cards ready."

I showed her the card I was given. "So, they're giving these to everyone?"

"No," she said after looking at it. "That's just for the 'boxers. The rest of the people they pretend to watch, and occasionally, they'll duck into an alley or something. It's totally adorable. I want to have a guy like that."

I shoved the card into my pocket. "It's awesome, let's just enjoy it! I wish I'd thought of something to do or dress up as." I was happy to see her look relaxed. She'd been so tense for weeks. I played with her phone in my pocket. I was about to report that the phone had been silent all day when a bunch of people dashed around the corner.

'What now?' I sighed.

Chapter Twenty-Two

An ambulance was pulling in just as we caught up to everyone. I breathed a sigh of relief when I accounted for Trace, Sean, and Nick. As the stretcher was loaded, I could see the top of a curly redhead.

"Is that Russ?" Trace asked, peering over heads on her tiptoes.

Sue was beside her with Ninja Turtle. "Yeah, he fell down the back staircase," Sue said. "Looks like he broke his leg. So much for his special stamps this weekend," Sue muttered.

Trace frowned at Sue. "I'm not sure that's what we should be worried about. I'm just glad it wasn't something even worse."

Ninja Turtle stayed silent, and I had a momentary realization that I still didn't know that man's real name.

"Right, of course. I just meant he'll be sad to not finish." Sue backtracked, flushed.

I looked around the area and didn't see anything he would have tripped over as he went down the stairs leading to the little park in the middle of town. "I should probably get to the hospital and keep him company. Make sure he gets back to the inn okay." I said.

"Zack already said he'd go," Sue said. "He was with him when he fell."

I peeked around and saw Zack settling into the back of the ambulance. I got his attention, and we did a few seconds of awkward charades where I tried to imply that I should go, and he waved me away.

The arrival of more EMTs into my life made me uneasy. Maybe we should cancel and send everyone home. Not that it would work. They already have the clues and the boxes. The best we could do is kick them out of Alice's, but I'm sure they'd find new places to bunk.

Sue opened her mouth to speak, but I interrupted. I just needed to stop for a bit. "Well, nothing more to see here. Where are you all off to 'box next?" I asked.

"Going to meet up with that group ahead," Trace said.

"I'll take Baron back so you can get into the buildings."

Trace knelt and let Baron give her a few good dog licks on the face before walking off, trailed by Ninja Turtle.

The rest of the assembled crowd returned to their regular business with the ambulance away and the excitement over. In moments, it didn't appear that anything had happened. The next group of 'boxers trekked past us into the museum. A few stopped to scratch Baron's head. I was left standing on the corner, unsure of what to do, when my stomach decided for me.

The vendor stalls were in full swing. I put my new T-shirt on over the cami I wore and went to stand in a depressingly long line for some BBQ.

"I hope he's going to be okay." I hadn't even noticed Sue had walked over with me. I nodded but was at the end of my ability to be social. I could use a break.

"Not to imply anything, but do you know anything about Fisherman or Night Hiker?" She asked.

"Why?" I hedged.

"They were both with him when he fell. Maybe they had a fight?" She nervously chewed on her fingernail while I absorbed what she said.

Nathan again. Who is this man, and why does he keep disappearing when I'm around? I didn't know Zack, but I hated to believe he was capable of that. Especially with the amount of time he's spent with Trace lately.

"I'm sure they would have spoken up if one of them saw the other push her down the stairs. It was an accident, but I'll talk to them if it makes you feel better." I said.

I didn't want to spend more time with Sue, or anyone, if I didn't need to. I was running on zero sleep, agitation, and fear. I needed protein and caffeine stat. I decided it was time for a food choice shift. "Oh look, I hadn't realized they had a Korean truck. I'm going to go check that out. See you back at the house!" I said, waving bye.

Well, it wasn't entirely a fabricated escape. I would take Korean BBQ bulgogi over pulled pork BBQ any day of the week, and I hadn't seen the truck before then. However, once I got my food, I discreetly checked where she was sitting before I picked a spot far away. I pulled up a chair at the cafe next door, ordered a Diet Coke, and confirmed it was okay to eat my lunch there as they didn't serve the food. Baron curled up beside me. The cafe won my eternal patronage when they brought him out a water bowl without me having to ask. When stuck on a puzzle, it's best to get your mind somewhere else. I settled in to read the book I'd picked up earlier. I hadn't bothered waiting in line for the signature.

I was about to savor my first bite when my pocked buzzed. Sighing, I put my fork down and dug for the phone. What was the purpose of trying to get away from it all when phone service seemed to be so darn reliable in town?

No caller ID came up, so I hesitated before saying hello. Silence.

"Well, that's rude. It's your turn to talk." I coaxed. The call went dead.

The bustling of families around me, eating and chatting was not enough to keep me from feeling exposed and alone. I was happy to have a large dog by my side.

I was still looking down at the phone when the text came through. 'Leave what's mine alone.' All thoughts of it being a harmless wrong number were out the window. I absentmindedly rubbed my palm and took deep breaths to settle my nerves.

Trace plopped down across from me, and I jumped a little in my seat. "Something you want to share with me?" She asked.

I looked from her to the phone and raised an eyebrow at her. I wasn't about to share that text with her yet. She waved my phone in front of me. "You got a few texts while I was phone sitting, my dear. Do you want the one from the adorable guy first?"

I used her phone to mark my spot in the book and grabbed my phone from her.

"Oh". The first text I saw was from Karen. 'Without a name or phone number to start with, there's not much for me to go on. Just keep taking notes on anything you think might be suspicious. I've shared everything with the deputies in your area.'

"We're sharing things with deputies now when we weren't even sure there was a 'this'? I could tell she was more embarrassed than angry, but she wasn't stupid.

"I think we can both agree that we have a 'this,' and we need everyone in the loop," I countered. "You know me. I'm an 'exhaust all possible avenues' kind of person. And maybe I've watched a few too many seasons of Criminal Minds, but you keep my phone for the weekend, and we'll see what happens with yours."

I tried to hand the phone back to her.

"Nyah-uh. You have one more text to read," Trace said in a sing-song voice. Her hand went up to play with her necklace out of habit, and I was crushed by the look on her face when it wasn't there.

I didn't recognize the next number, but the text was from Nick asking if I'd like to help with a bonus clue he received.

The fact he had my number wasn't surprising as it was part of the packet for people heading here for the weekend in case they got lost. What a joke that was. They would have had more luck giving me directions. I smiled that he had thought of me.

I copied the phone number down in case I wanted to respond. Sue, Clara, and Chris came by. "Trace, want to come to the next stop with us," Sue asked.

Clara opened her logbook. "Halfway done with finding the aliens." She leaned in, lowering her dark sunglasses. "Want to give me a hint as to where the boss alien is?" She asked.

"Alien? I KNEW IT! You're working with them." An older man sporting a camouflage vest and khaki pants stomped up to us, his finger pointed at Clara.

"Woah," I said, holding up my hands. "This is just a game we're playing." But he'd already made the mistake of reaching out and grabbing Sue's arm.

I could have told him not to do that. Trace had his arm pulled up behind his back, and he was on the ground faster than I could warn him. After a second, she let go and stepped back, immediately ready to help him up to his feet. He scooted away from her on his butt. The others had taken a few steps away from us.

"You're crazy," he said. "But I'll find out what you're doing. You're not going to get me again." Once he scuttled backward like a crab about five feet, he returned to his feet and left.

"Where did you learn that?" Sue asked.

"Remi and I took some self-defense classes last year," Trace said.

"Feeling a little trigger-happy?" I asked, giving her a quick, one-armed hug.

She shrugged. "A little spooked still, I guess. I'm, erm, glad you texted those people now. "Thanks." She hugged me quickly. "You'll make sure that guy is okay?" she asked.

"You just keep working on the buddy system this weekend, and no heading off somewhere dark and spooky on your own."

She hmphed at me but nodded before heading off to catch up with the group heading into the bakery.

"Buy me another chocolate marshmallow alien!" I yelled after her. The people around me stared. "I, uh, really like them."

I debated getting back into the book, but I wasn't in the right mindset. What I needed to do was get back on the case and find Nathan. I'd also seen the alien guy enter the bookstore and figured I'd better check on him. Didn't want him pressing charges or causing an issue of this. I had a feeling I'd just met the mysterious other Chuck.

Aliens, crackpots, stalkers, letterboxers. The town was packed with people, and until this mystery with Trace was figured out, I didn't trust any of them.

With her safely off, I made sure Baron knew to stay, and I popped back into the bookstore and walked over to the owner. The bookstore owner confirmed my suspicion when I pointed Chuck out in the crowd. I explained what had happened.

"I'll talk to him," the bookstore owner said. "Can't guarantee he'll listen or understand, but he'll probably spend tomorrow at home. Usually, one day of being around people is all he can handle."

The number of things I should do was starting to feel too overwhelming to tackle. I went back out to Baron, sipping on my drink. I have a lost necklace and an elusive person, but I'm surrounded by people whose whole mission this weekend was to find things. I sent out a message to the event group about getting two bonus stamps. I had several extra alien duck stamps that I hadn't hid for the weekend. Alright, Nathan. Try to hide from me now.

Chapter Twenty-Three

A small step towards fixing things. Now for a harder one as I spied Bob across the road. It spoke to the gravity of the situation that I waved at him to come over and join me.

As he pulled out a chair, I jumped right in.

"Look. First, I need you to send Sean home." I took a deep breath before the next part. "Then I need you to do me a favor." I hated asking, but despite his player ways, he'd worked in personal security. If anyone could keep her safe, it would be him. "You can stay, but I need you to keep an eye on Trace for me. There's some creep after her."

Trace was not his favorite person, but he was all business when it came to safety. "What level of creep are we talking about?" He asked.

"Level red as far as I'm concerned. Someone followed her here from home after a month of silent cell phone calls." I filled him in with what little I knew.

There was no way Trace would agree to stay locked in a room at the inn for the rest of the weekend, so plan B was to surround her with as many eyes as possible. There was still the possibility that this was all Bob's doing, but that didn't feel right. And I knew there was no way Trace would allow herself to be in a room with Bob alone.

He nodded and started off in her direction. "Remi, take photos of crowds near here whenever you can. I'll do the same. We can pull them up tonight and see if we notice anyone who seems to always be hovering around. The average person wouldn't be in more than one or two places this group goes."

Solid thought. Knowing where the clues would take them, I decided to meet them at the next location. See who was there and who came by. First, I set Trace's phone to camera mode and took as many pictures as I could around me.

I was going to get my steps in today. Thankfully, the next stop got us a bit away from the crowds. The bank and the jail were in a small park in the older part of the town. Other than the two small old stone buildings, there was a playground, canon, and a few metal placards telling about the history. Trace was heading in with a small group of people I didn't know as I arrived. The previous group was already rushing over to the jail cell. The clue for that was vague, as there wasn't much left in the cell. It said simply, "*This is where bank robbers will end up but will have trouble resting.*" It wouldn't take them long to find the stamp under the cot in the cell.

I walked to where I saw Chelsea by the bank. She had traded her zebra top for a Historical Irving Volunteer t-shirt but had supplemented her outfit with a pair of Martian antennas. "You've done a great job. We've raised quite a bit towards repairs today." She said

"I hadn't realized you were one of the volunteers. I appreciate you letting us go in all these buildings and play."

"Are you planning more things like this when you get your place running?" She asked, accepting a donation from another letterboxer.

I shook my head in dismay, remembering how many hoops I still needed to jump through. "Not if Mary has anything to say about it."

"Hon, you get yourself set, and that'll work itself out. These shops and the town need people, or it'll die off. There are already too many shops having to close. Besides, life's too short to be super serious." She motioned towards my new shirt.

I smiled and left to explore the little park. So many things had gone wrong, but all around me were people taking silly pictures and having a fantastic time. It was hard to tell the UFO attendees from the letterboxers as they seemed to have joined forces in celebrating both.

I fit right in, taking photos. And I thought I played the part of a tourist well.

"How is it that Bob is on the same clue path as me?" Trace asked, joining up with me.

I shrugged. "Must have been a mistake when I rushed the extra clues this morning."

"Get up on the canon with us, Trace!" a lady in a Ghostbuster outfit yelled down. "Can you take a photo?" She asked me, holding out her phone.

Happy to avoid Trace's suspicious glance, I helped them take a few more silly photos. I caught Bob's eye, and he shook his head. He had this area covered, so I decided to tackle another area. Two streets down, I was happy to see someone leave the nondescript office where my lawyer did business from. It had been shuttered tight the past few times I'd swung by. Well, I was happy until the person crossed the street and I saw it was Mary. I'd best go in and see what new roadblock I have.

"Ah, Ms. McKenna. Are you enjoying the festivities?" Stan, the lawyer, greeted me as I walked in. The inside of the office was decorated tastefully but with restraint. No cute knick-knacks or family photos.

"Yes, lovely town. I was wondering if there was any, um, news?" I asked.

He tapped a blue file folder on his desk. "The pest control agency advised me the tenting will be down tomorrow night as planned."

I smiled. "That's great news, but I was wondering more about permits?"

He took a sip from his coffee mug while I awaited my fate.

"That decision will take some time." He hedged. "There have been several outside parties and a few members of the council concerned with the addition of another BnB and the type of tourists your establishment will bring to town. They are causing delays in the permit approvals."

I looked out his window to the street as a man painted green walked by, an alien-shaped stuffed toy in his hand.

"Is there anything I can do about Mary gunning for me?" I asked bluntly.

"While I am pleased she has risen up to take interest in her role, her fervid campaigning against you has been quite unexpected. I am investigating precedents for the zoning, and I will provide all that I can to assist. It would take a majority of the vote, so if at least three vote in your favor, there won't be an issue."

Okay, I'll add win over three council members to my list of things to get done. No problem. "One other thing. Where can I buy a metal detector?"

Chapter Twenty-Four

A few hours of scouring trails I knew Trace had been in left me a few coins and bottle caps richer but no necklace in sight. I hiked the metal detector onto my shoulder and checked my texts. One from Trace saying she was back and was stealing my tub for a long soak. One was Sue asking if I was night hiking later, and then one was Nick responding to me about doing the Monster Duck loop trail.

Having Trace in my room meant I had to have my super-secret meeting in her room.

A knock on the door had me up in seconds. It had been a long time since I was pleased to see Bob. "Hurry up and get in here," I said.

I had my laptop up with the photos already loaded. His gaze lingered too long at my legs, but one look at my face put him back in work mode. Bob brought up his pictures on his laptop so we could compare.

Nada. No one stood out. Where is the 'ah hah' moment photo they always have in crime shows of someone looking creepy in a ball cap?

"I'll keep an eye on her tomorrow, too." He said as he was leaving. "But she's not going to like it. You need to tell her." He cautioned.

"If I tell her, she'll like it even less." I knew he was right. It just annoyed me to admit it.

A few moments after he closed the door, Trace's phone buzzed with a text. "Keep Bob away from her."

I rushed to open the door, but no one was in the hallway. I turned and saw that we would have been silhouetted on the blinds with the room lights on. Anyone outside may have seen us being very close. I turned off the lights and pulled the shades aside to look out. The grounds were crowded with people. I knew Trace was taking a bath in my room, but I was the only one who knew that.

I saved a screenshot and sent it to Bob to warn him our stalker may consider him somewhat of a threat and to be on guard. I winced at his response.

'I knew you cared.'

I walked downstairs to find the front door wide open with people wandering in and out of the dining room. I peeked in. A chest full of ice and drinks sat on the large oak dining room table. Alice was setting down an urn of coffee beside it with paper cups.

"Alice, every time I see you, you're in the midst of some new organizational nightmare. What the heck is going on?"

She gestured outside to show all the people on the front lawn. "Those are folks from Jason's astronomy club. And, of course, all the letterboxers." She scanned the grounds a bit more. "A few people from town. Maybe nearby towns?" She shrugged. "We have prime sky real estate up here, away from the town's lights. I normally wouldn't have them over while we had guests, but…"

"No, I get it. It's an exciting night in the stars with the meteor shower and the UFO news. To be honest, I'm looking forward to watching the meteors myself. Do you think Jason would let me look through his telescope?" I asked

"Of course but go at your own risk. Once that group spots a potential convert, you may have difficulty escaping."

Car lights caught my attention, and I watched a car inch its way up the driveway.

"What are they looking for?" I asked out loud, suspicious of any newcomer. I needed some sleep. My mood towards people wasn't fully rational.

The car parked, and boxes full of pizza spewed from the backseat into the waiting arms of letterboxers. Nearby, Jake and Chelsea had set up a small tent and were selling pie slices.

Standing next to the pizza table, Russ leaned on some crutches. He taped a gluten-free sign under two of the boxes. Relieved and a little guilty I hadn't thought to check on him earlier, I went to see him.

"Glad to see you up and about! What happened?" I asked as my stomach growled. The earlier bulgogi in town was long behind me. He handed me a paper plate, and I added a few veggie supreme slices.

"I've never been called graceful." He mumbled around some pizza. "Some of us stopped for coffee and coming down the spiral stairs was too much for my knee, I guess. One second I'm chatting with Nathan and the next I'm staring up at Zack." He lightly tapped the cast on his right foot with the crutch. "At least all I did was break an ankle." He said.

"Well, I'm glad to have you back. Go put that leg up and rest."

"Hey, Remi! Come sit with us." You don't know how much of the middle schooler you still have in you until it's time to find a place to sit with a bunch of people you don't know. I accepted the invitation and pulled up a spot of grass with Chris and Clara.

Clara spoke up. "We've been hoping to get an exchange with you, but we were having so much fun in town that we didn't get a chance."

I wiped my hands on the napkin and pulled out my logbook, stamp, and ink pad. "Happy to. As I flipped the logbook open, I saw the earlier notes from the ducks in my room and figured it was prime time to work more on the clue.

"You're all staying in the inn, aren't you? Anyone want to talk about ducks?" I asked. I could see the lights come on inside them. They were ready to see what I had.

They had the words 'washing' and 'corn'.

"I think we're still missing a relevant clue somewhere. I keep wondering if we're meant to combine the clues or not. If the prize is one weekend's stay, there's no way to divide that between the whole group. And I can't see Alice hoping we'll all backstab each other to secretly get to the prize first." I said.

Alice came over, a slice of mushroom pizza in one hand. "Now, I didn't say there was only one prize for the winner. Maybe there are two locations. Maybe each of your clues will work on its own. Hard to say. Enjoy!" She kept walking towards Jason and his group as they surrounded a second telescope being set up on the lawn.

"Look! The meteor shower is starting," Jason yelled.

I leaned back in the grass and put my hands behind my head. At first, there was only one every minute or so, but then streaks started showing up constantly. The stars were so much brighter than back home. The streaks across the sky made a beautiful night display.

I sensed someone lying down next to me on the grass. I smiled and turned my head, hoping it was Nick. It was Bob.

"I'm not here to cause problems. Just enjoying the show with you."

I sighed and tuned him out, watching the natural fireworks until I drifted off. I woke to find someone had covered me with a blanket, and my new companion was Nick.

"Hey, sleepy. Bob went to drop off Sean, so I told him I'd stay with you a bit. Didn't want to wake you. You seemed exhausted."

Excellent. I wiped the drool from my mouth and oomphed my way to a seated position. "Thanks, but my body didn't find the ground that comfortable."

I stretched out my back and looked around, a little disoriented. Jason was arguing with a guy in his group about one of the streaks they saw. The shape was different and had a 'weird arc.' The last bit was accompanied by finger quotes. I looked up and saw the sky had returned to normal.

"There's only going to be a few every hour now. Happy to keep you company if you wanted to stay outside and watch." Nick said.

I waved off his hand as I stood and wiped some grass and dirt off me. "I have to find Trace."

"Ok, I never heard back on if you wanted to do that box with me." He asked.

My brain was focused on how to tell Trace I'd assigned Bob as a watchdog. "Yeah, no, that sounds good. Let's plan for tomorrow morning?" I yelled back as I went towards Trace's group.

She wasn't far away, curled up on a camp chair near Zack, Alice, Sue, and Russ. Russ has his leg propped up on an old log. Baron's chin was resting beside it.

Alice waved me to sit beside her and leaned in towards me. Trace was on my other side, deep in conversation with Zack.

"I wanted to let you know I was planning on going out with everyone tomorrow, and I'll make sure I'm in Trace's group," Alice whispered to me.

"You are a rockstar, Alice. Oh, have you heard any more about Scott? I asked.

"Nothing from the Sheriff so far. I was talking with people from town, and no one seems to know how he got here or why he'd even be here. Jason did pop over to the fire station for a shift. The word there is that the car may have been tampered with. The wiring was a mess."

"That would be why the Sheriff made a point to mention I was near the scene." I muttered. Scott's murder and the one from Trace's apartment ate away at me. I knew crazy stuff happened all the time, but why now?

I waited for a break in Trace's conversation to tell her what had happened today. Well, what I had done today. She went from alarmed to pissed off in zero seconds.

"BOB," she said, looking at me, her voice raised. Everyone nearby turned to look at us.

"Yes, I know. I had Bob look after you today and," I stressed quietly, "If you insist on going out tomorrow, he will be there again. That should make it hugely clear to you how far I'll go to keep you safe."

She sighed but didn't argue. "I can't live like this," she said. "When the weekend is over, there will be no more babysitter."

I was going to allow her that belief for now. "Deal. Tonight, let's go enjoy looking for spaceships."

"I'm going off on a hike." Her lips were pressed together, ready to argue. "With a bunch of others. I'll take Baron."

"Oh, great. What's he going to do? Mark the person with fur or snuggle them to death?"

"You and I are the only ones who know he has all the protective qualities of a teddy bear," she said.

She was right. I've seen burly men cross to the other side of the street from me while walking Baron. I handed Trace his leash and the extra pepper spray I had in my bag.

Trace glared at me when Bob walked up and joined us. I was relieved Sean had left. I hadn't been surprised to see some of the other families leave already. Things were a mess. I scanned the lawn. With the light coming off all the flashlights, it wasn't much of a night walk. I've seen cloudy days with less light coverage.

"Don't worry, hon. The set they're after is just on the farm's perimeter, and Jason is on lookout duty." Alice said, pointing to the roof. Jason and others had moved up there to gather around the much larger telescope.

I waited on the porch and watched as the bobbing lights of their flashlights disappeared into the tree line. Ten minutes later, no other lights followed, so I relaxed a little.

"I didn't think your friend and Bob would become a thing," Nick said as he joined me.

I burst out laughing at the idea of Bob and Trace together before realizing he was scowling. "What makes you think that?" I looked at Nick.

"Must have heard someone mention it." He shrugged, looking out towards the various groups. "After what you told me about Bob, I was just surprised she's allowing him around."

"Yeah, well, so is she. Trust me." I took a deep breath in and out and physically forced my shoulders down. "I gotta take care of some stuff."

"You're a hard person to convince to stick around." He joked.

"I can't even begin to explain how complicated this weekend has become."

Chapter Twenty-Five

Feeling Nick's eyes on me, I abandoned him again. Some fun I was. Passing through the kitchen to head upstairs to my room, I noticed Alice moving a chalkboard into the corner of the room.

"Could I borrow that tonight?" I asked.

"The chalkboard? Sure." She dug through a junk drawer and handed me an assortment of chalk colors. "I plan on using it to list food choices for breakfast, but that doesn't count for this weekend. Something I can help with?"

"I want to see if I can figure something out." I mainly wanted her to think I was trying to solve her puzzle or someone else's. No one needed to know I wanted to play detective and create a murder board.

I cleared off my dresser in my room and leaned the chalk-board against the wall. I started a timeline. There had to be a clue as to who was doing all this to Trace.

She had first mentioned the phone calls a month ago. They started out infrequently, at odd hours of the night. She proba-bly wasn't even sure when they started because, for a while, she blew them off as drunk, misdialed calls. I tried going through her phone from the day she started receiving the strange calls and marking down all the incoming calls from blocked num-bers with dates and times. They were all over the place. No set time to work with. I didn't know which ones were spam and which were creeps, so I went with the first day she texted me about it.

I added Scott's accident, his death, and Russ's injury. With every ounce of my being, I wanted to not have any of those connected to Trace, but I had a feeling I was being naive.

I pulled up my laptop and found Trace's Facebook page. She posted a lot, but this way, I could see if she'd added anyone new lately or if anyone was in her face about anything. Then I checked her cat café's website for comments. Zip. Nothing seemed out of the ordinary. Her last boyfriend's status was in a relationship, and the profile pic was of him with some brunette. It didn't look like he was holding out hope to reconcile.

I wanted to crush the chalk, but that would just make a mess on the carpet for Alice to deal with. I had nothing to go on. Biting my lip, I Googled stalking again, this time focusing on the behav-iors and escalations. After about ten minutes, I realized sleeping tonight would be difficult. I texted Trace a quick check-in request and felt relieved at her thumbs-up reply.

Stalking was more prevalent than I'd ever thought possible. The internet had increased the ability for people to gain personal details about others to base their fantasies on. I jotted down some notes to share with Trace on keeping personal information more secure and ways to keep track of what was going on. I grabbed a blank logbook from my bag and transferred all the information with times and dates when possible so I could add notes as I went. Trace would need to fill in anything else that came to mind and keep track of what she saw. If we were going to get this scumbag, it was going to be with facts.

I heard a distant "woof" and checked outside to see flashlights bobbing in the distance. I went out to the porch. Trace let Baron off his leash, and he came barreling at me but stopped and went into a polite sit, waiting for head rubs.

"A welcoming committee?" Trace asked, a tinge of annoyance in her tone.

"How were the 'boxes?" I asked, ignoring Trace's comment.

"I loved the one about the duck autopsy!" Zack spoke up.

"Yeah, that and the abduction one were fantastic," someone else added. "Hey do we get the stamp for sightings of Nathan?"

I zeroed in on that last bit. "Where was he?"

"He was putting the last box back when we got there. I grabbed a pic of him, but he rushed off." She showed me the shot.

It wasn't going to help me get ahold of him, but at least I knew people were on the lookout. If he was a problem, I can only hope that helped. I handed her the special stamp as Bob came over.

Bob came up to join the group. "My favorite was the frog."

"There wasn't a frog," Sue said.

Trace glared at Bob. "I might have stuck my hand into a tree and yelped when a frog jumped onto it."

Zack laughed. "I think we can safely call it a scream."

"It startled me!" Trace had no trouble laughing at herself.

I couldn't help smiling. "And no one has a video to show me? I'm disappointed! Quick, let's go back and try to recapture it."

Trace gently punched me in the shoulder. "Be nice. Or I will replace you with Zack as my personal letterboxing companion. Not only does he 'box in style," she motioned towards his kilt. "But he found the box even though it had been moved. High five." Zack and Trace slapped hands.

"I guess no mothership landed to take over on the lawn?" Bob sneered towards the group on the roof.

"If they did, I'd be sure and send them straight to you so you wouldn't miss out." I turned my back on him to talk to Trace. "Are you calling it a night? I have some stuff I want to go over with you."

She didn't seem fooled by my nonchalant tone but waved goodbye to her group and followed me to my room.

Trace looked at the chalkboard and crossed her arms, slightly hunching her shoulders. "I'm not going to hide from this."

"'This is the opposite of hiding. We're going to Nancy Drew this thing. I need you to write down everything that seemed odd or anything you can remember being out of place."

"Fine. Give me a second to wash my hands. I was just attacked by a frog after all."

I nodded solemnly and handed her the chalk when she came back. She tapped the chalk on the board a few times lost in thought before listing packages that have gone missing and a few calls at work that she hadn't mentioned before. "There's probably more, but it's not like I kept a log."

"Let's do that starting now. Overkills is better than not having enough info." I said.

"Fine, I'll keep track, but are you still keeping my phone?"

"Probably best unless you want to deal with the incoming texts."

As I said that, I realized the last text I got was from the stalker directly to me.

We heard a scream through the window and froze.

Chapter Twenty-Six

Trace and I grabbed our flashlights and ran outside. Lights popped up all over the yard from cellphones and other flashlights. With everyone running around, it was impossible to tell what was going on. It was a chaotic display of light and sound.

"Are they here? Did they land?"

"Oh my God, what happened."

"They found a body by the lake."

"Was it them? Are they still here?"

Suddenly, a light the size of a small spotlight lit the entire front acreage, causing us to throw our hands over our eyes. It silenced the group for a moment.

"Okay, everyone, calm down," Jason yelled from behind the light. "I need to know if someone is hurt."

Someone yelled from the left corner of the yard near the lake. "Please help. I think he's dead."

"Call 911 and bring my bag," Jason yelled. Alice ran into the house. The landlines would be far more reliable than a cell signal.

Jason ran down the slight hill towards the lake. "Everyone step away and let us have some space."

We all crowded behind him but kept about six feet open, so we weren't breathing down his neck. "Hold up your lights to cover the lake area," he instructed.

My eyes watered from the intensity of everyone with a light helping to light the area like it was daylight. I saw Sue kneeling beside Bob, who was half lying in the lake. Bob was on his side, and Sue seemed to be trying to push the water from his lungs.

Jason rushed down beside her and searched for Bob's pulse. Sue pulled her knees up to her chest and hugged them, crying. "I saw him lying there in the lake and went to check on him. I tried to pull him out, but he was so heavy, I fell in with him." Jason waved another person over, and together, they pulled Bob's body entirely from the coarse grasses around the lake. "I need some blankets!" he yelled, as he started to examine Bob for injuries. There was blood on the side of his shirt, but no obvious wound I could see.

A small group of people ran for their tents and returned in seconds with an assortment of sleeping bags and blankets to wrap him in. Someone put a blanket around Sue, and she clasped it with both hands close to her body, despite the warmth of the evening.

Alice appeared next to Jason, and I heard him whisper to her. "Just in case, don't let anyone leave. I'm not sure this was an accident."

"Is he.."

He shook his head. "No, but he's in shock and the head wound needs to be seen to."

She nodded and started towards the front iron gate. "I'll go direct the ambulance."

And to make sure no other cars head out, I thought to myself. Trying to help, I called people to action. "Why don't you, you and you stay here to help light the area and get everyone else out of the way, back up towards the house." My voice shook a little, and I worried if he was okay. Was this my fault for getting him involved?

Trace started to help me corral them. "Come on, everyone. The best thing we can do is stay out of the way."

"When can we turn off all these lights again?" Charlie asked as he gazed at the night sky.

"Seriously? I think we have more important things to worry about right now." I snapped.

"Have you thought maybe they did this to him?" He spat. "He was so against the visitors. He was harassing us at the town museum yesterday, calling us all crazy. Maybe they decided to teach him a lesson."

Trace got right up into his face. "If this was done by someone, it was human." She pointed her finger at him. "Maybe a human who cared more about visitors than their own kind. Where have you been all night?"

He stuttered and backed away from the ferocity in her expression. "I only left the telescope after that crazy lady screamed. We all ran down. Just ask any of them."

I grabbed Trace's arm and pulled her towards the inn.

"I'll 'visitor' his face if he causes any more problems," she snarled.

"Woah there, slugger. What has gotten into you? Normally, you're the one talking me off the ledge."

She collapsed into a nearby camp chair and put her head into her hands. "I can't take any more. First, the calls, the notes, the injuries. Everything. People are heading to the hospital left and right. What is going on? It's like everything is falling apart everywhere I go."

I knelt next to her and took her hands in mine. "Hey, we will figure this out. I already started with the notes, and I'm assuming everything is connected until we know otherwise."

She looked up at me.

"I'm not saying it is one hundred percent, but let's look at this logically and see if we can find an answer. If someone is doing these things, we have seen them. They may be here even now. Let's figure out who and put a stop to this. The Sheriff hasn't been doing anything that I can see except bug you."

While we were talking, I saw the ambulance arrive, and once again, a person was heading off on a gurney. "Someone should go with him," Trace said, getting up. I pushed her gently back down, shocked that she would even volunteer.

"Jason has this, and I promise I will check on him later. You need to get some rest." I said. "I'll wait here."

Once the ambulance left, I saw Alice and the police close the iron gates at the end of the driveway and lock them. I was not sure I liked the idea of being trapped on the property with someone capable of drowning people. Still, I knew she was trying to be as cautious as possible.

"Come on, let's go back to my room." Once upstairs, I pulled out the chalkboard again. "Okay, we need to figure out what these have to do with each other. Let's start with Scott's death."

Trace took a deep breath. "We don't know for sure the car accident wasn't an accident. It could have been squirrels that chewed through the wiring. After that, he could have gotten turned around and landed here."

"So, let's recap. You think it was a freak squirrel accident and a fit of amnesia where he then randomly came here to die?" I looked at her for a beat.

"Well, when you phrase it like that, I guess not. What does he have to do with me?"

"Because some random guy hits on you, and then suddenly he's dead in the garden? You can't buy that as a coincidence. He was already hitting on his next victim. It could be a simple case of a jealous boyfriend, but he's staying." I said.

"If we're including everything, you're forgetting one incident." Trace went over and wrote 'neighbor' on the board. "If we're going to science, we have to add all possibilities. I don't believe in this many coincidences, either," she said, sounding defeated.

"Good! Yes, let's start there." I put the header Victims over "neighbor" and started a second column of "suspects."

A knock at the door stopped me before I could get the first name down. I threw a towel over the chalkboard. It would be too much to try to explain.

Nathan stood there, his hands in his pockets. "I think it's time we talked."

I opened the door wider so he could Trace was behind me. He nodded at her and didn't seem upset that I wasn't alone. That was one check in his favor.

"Well, we can talk fine right here at the door," I said.

He nodded and even took a step backward to give me more space.

"Ever since you sent out the note asking for people to find me, I've wanted to come clear the air, but Bob insisted he needed more time."

I closed my eyes and took a deep breath. Of course, this was Bob's doing. "What's the con?" I asked bluntly.

"Hey, no. I'm not a con man. I'm a real estate developer. Bob hired me to come out and lay out plans for a place he would get soon. He said there was complications, and he wanted me to pretend to fit in while things worked out." Nathan shrugged. "So I went with camping, and then honestly, I was having fun until he asked me to make myself scarce."

Nathan moved forward slightly but not enough to cause alarm. "But the things that have been going on around here," He gestured around himself, "are too much. I did not sign up for this, and I am out. I wanted to make sure you knew before I left. Oh, and could you call off the hunt for me to get the bonus stamp? I feel like I'm on the run trying to avoid those boxers. They are relentless."

We stayed silent a moment after Nathan left. Then I removed the towel from the board and wrote Bob under both Victim and Suspect. Earlier today, I would never have believed him capable of harming someone, but maybe this con had gone so wrong that he crossed a line. Russ went under both as well. Risking a small injury to throw people off wasn't too much of a stretch.

Trace wrote Zack on the board. "He's been a total sweetheart, but he is new to this, and he's been spending a lot of time with me.

I added Nick below that. "No one ever mentions how hard it is to suspect people you want to call your friend," I said, adding Chris and Clara as well.

I stepped back and tried to take it all in when my phone rang. Trace grabbed it from her back pocket and answered.

"It's Jason," she said. "Uh-huh. Yes. Okay. I understand." Her mood was going downhill with each word she uttered.

After she hung up, she seemed broken. "I'm sorry, Rem," she said. "Jason says they found my necklace in Bob's pocket. The Sheriff is heading upstairs to talk to us."

I was both broken by yet another betrayal and horrified that I had trusted him to watch Trace for me. But why? What possible motive would Bob have to hurt these people? Scaring me out of town and hoping I'd sell dirt cheap?

My bedroom was starting to feel like Grand Central Station. I opened the door and left it that way as I added more notes to the board. Sheriff Marrow walked in and approached us.

"Again, with the mighty speedy police work," I tried to joke.

"I was on my way home when I got the call from the hospital. This type and amount of violence is a first for this area. I want to get to the bottom of it as quickly as possible. The number of small-time issues with over-drinking and brawling are already keeping the patrols busy, thanks to all that alien nonsense." He wiped his brow, looked over, and saw our notes on the chalkboard. "What's this?" He asked.

"We were trying to get to the bottom of whoever was stalking Trace." I sighed. "Unfortunately, it looks like now we know."

He went over and took a few moments to read through it. "You're saying all this is connected?" His brow furrowed.

"Who knows anymore? Scott is a stretch, but like you, we figured there were too many coincidences around us to ignore it."

Trace nodded, her expression settling into despair.

"Your friend Bob is in pretty bad shape. Sue is staying at the hospital with him. If he's the problem, what happened to him?" He asked.

I debated arguing the friend part but didn't have the energy left to care.

"Maybe he was trying to do something by the lake, slipped and hit his head," I said, putting my chalk down. "Or what if this was Nathan?" I asked before filling in Morrow with his earlier visit.

"Their deal went sideways, and he needed to cover his tracks before he left? He was in a hurry to get out of here."

Sheriff Morrow sent a quick message on his radio to see if Bob was talking and to try and get Nathan before he left.

"Stalkers tend to be much closer to the people they are trying to be near. It allows them the illusion that they are part of their stalkee's life. Is there anyone that you seem to see around everywhere you go?" He asked.

Trace shook her head. "No one stands out. Honestly, with my work and volunteer hours, I don't tend to go out much anyway unless it's to the movies or Remi's place."

Morrow's phone buzzed with an incoming text as I was about to add more names. I looked down at my ink-stained fingers and remembered manicured hands. I blame poor sleep and stress. I knew who Trace's shadow was. The only person who knew I had Trace's phone and used it to text me.

"You need to keep Sue at the hospital," I said

Chapter Twenty-Seven

Six am and I was awake. My head ached and my mind wouldn't stop trying to figure out where Sue was. She had gotten out of the hospital before the deputies arrived. I was not fully conscious or mobile but awake enough to know that going back to sleep was no longer on the agenda.

I quickly scanned the room, wondering what had startled me awake. Trace had put her foot down about sleeping in her own room last night, so she wasn't the culprit. The door was locked, and I didn't hear any movement from the rest of the house. I turned my head and saw a folded piece of paper from the light under the door. I debated staying in my safe blanket cocoon, but curiosity beat out the fluffy comforter. The paper was cream-colored card stock and printed inside '*Let's meet at your place for our hike. Nick*'

Baron must have given a small 'woof' when the paper appeared and woke me up. I groaned and flopped back into bed. Last night's craziness had erased my plans to head out with him today. The Sheriff had tried to get Sue detained at the hospital, but she was long gone by the time anyone went to look for her. The things she'd left here in the barn were some clothes and toiletries she'd easily do without. What she hadn't left was a manifesto on what brought all this on. Why Trace? The police left someone in the house with us last night as a precaution, but they believed she was long gone by now.

"What do you think, Baron? Walk?"

He got up and stretched out his front legs. Once out of bed, there was no point in trying to get comfy again, so I went ahead and showered before heading down for a warm, caffeinated beverage. It felt like the first hint of Fall was coming in, so I grabbed a hoodie and giggled when Baron plopped his head down with an 'oomph.'

"I haven't forgotten you, boy." I picked up his leash from the floor, and my large fluff was at my side in seconds.

My hand was inches from knocking on Trace's door but I thought better of it. She was not a morning person, and she'd still be sleeping when I got back. I tried the door and confirmed it was locked. There was no way to be ninja stealthy with Baron's claws clicking on the wooden stairs, but hopefully, we wouldn't wake anyone. From the kitchen, I heard some humming and doors opening. I peeked in, not wanting to intrude.

"Morning, sweetie. Did you sleep okay?" Alice asked.

I hadn't noticed before, but Alice had a bit of Southern seeping out.

"Pull up a chair. Jason is on the roof, and it's good to have a bit of company when cooking." She noticed my furry companion and pointed towards the door. "Baron can hang out by the door." She said.

I was thankful she left it to me to broach the subject of Bob or Sue or anything about the past two days. I wasn't ready.

She filled a water bowl and put it on a footstool so Baron wouldn't have to bend down so far to get it. I loved considerate dog people. I added a bowl filled with his canned food.

"Jason went up this early?" I asked as I pulled up a stool to the counter and took the offered bowl of strawberries. They were smaller than I usually get but explosions of perfection. "Oh my God, these are yummy. Now I just need some warm chocolate to dip them in, and I'm set."

"I have a little greenhouse that I've been trying to use more, and the strawberries seem to be thriving." She laughed. "But Jason. No, he's late. Hasn't come back in yet, the silly man. He decided to sleep up there in case the "visitors" were seen." Alice winked at me when she made air quotes around "visitors." "It makes him happy, and it's harmless enough. By next week, he'll probably be scouring the woods for Bigfoot's cousin or a lake monster. I'll take it over football Sundays."

I smiled, enjoying her joyous energy. I hoped one day to have a relationship like hers. Everyone allowed their own brand of crazy with support from the other. But my partner would have to be the cook because I could never make muffins that smelled as good as the ones Alice was pulling out of the oven. Pumpkin and ginger filled the room, and I did all but drool as I stared at them.

"Now, now, these need to cool a bit, but I'll be sure to save you one." She looked at my backpack and back to me.

I held up my fingers silently, asking for two to be saved.

"Honey, are you sure it's a good idea to head out?" She asked

"The phone is charged. I have some pepper spray and Baron with me. If I see anything that seems off, I will hightail it back to you and your muffins. The Sheriff thinks she's hit the road, and I can't stay inside forever."

"Alright then but let me know when you're back." She wiped her hands on her apron and turned off the oven. "I've noticed Nick is an early riser as well. Maybe you can still get a clear head with some company." She said.

I looked at her, but she was all innocence and light, moving muffins to the cooling rack. I was surrounded by matchmakers.

"He is exactly who Baron and I are heading over to meet."

He wagged his butt at the sound of his name. A teethy yawn wafted canned dog food breath our way.

"Ugh, at least that helped me lose my appetite for now," I complained.

I debated trying to grab a muffin from the rack anyway, but Alice watched as we headed out. She must be used to having kids around with her inner sense of protecting the goods from wandering hands.

Soft snoring came from the tents as I eased through the sliding glass doors. They were sleeping in after their late night of meteors and attempted murder.

"You're heading out early," Ninja Turtle said as he unzipped his tent door. "Secret box?"

"No, a quick walk for Baron," I said, stepping away. After his weird behavior with Trace yesterday, I still doubted him. Even if he had been letterboxing for years.

He started to put on his hiking boots. "Let me come along. Is Trace coming, too?" He looked up at me as he asked.

"I appreciate the offer, but we're just going for a morning walk alone." I stressed the 'alone' and kept backing up towards the path. "Thanks, though." I waved goodbye before heading into the woods. Once I was out of his sight, I made sure my emergency whistle was packed. If I needed help, they should be able to hear the whistle back at the inn.

After five minutes, the overwhelming solitude and quiet of the forest around me had me wondering if this was a bright idea. I'd spent so much time telling Trace to travel with people, and here I was, completely ignoring my advice.

'That's it. Time to call this in as a bad idea and head back, Baron.' I shoved the clues in my pocket, packed up my compass, and jumped about a foot in the air when a hand landed on my shoulder.

"Sue! You scared me half to death!" I put my hand on my chest to keep my heart from leaping out. Horror movies are not my thing, but I don't generally scare easily. I looked at the trail around us and couldn't believe I hadn't heard her coming up behind me.

"I've been waiting for you." She was still and serious. "I should have known it would take you forever to leave bed and come out here. And you had to bring that dog."

Forever? Really? The sun was still yawning at me. Her derision over my sleeping habits was the least of my worries. She already had a few bodies under her belt.

"How did you know I'd be here?" I asked, stalling.

She looked down at me with evident disappointment in her eyes. "I left the note for you after I heard you yell the morning's plans to your little boyfriend. He is currently walking to meet you in the completely opposite direction."

"Oh, look, I appreciate you wanting to head out with me, but I was just going to head to the inn." I backed up, but she followed.

She edged a little closer, invading deep into my personal space bubble. "I agree with you that it's time you left. You should have left long ago. You hold her back, and you can't protect her. Only I can. Trying to get her to move out here where it's obviously not safe. You're not worth her time."

"What are you talking about?" My voice going up an octave. I tried to keep up the pretense that I didn't know, but acting wasn't my strong suit. I tried to move away again, but her hand came up and sprayed me in the face with what felt like liquid fire.

I flailed my arms, trying to create a zone around me to keep her back, but she threw a rope around my neck and tugged. I dropped to the ground, my head striking a small rock. I clawed at the rope, but she yanked it tighter.

"You can get up and walk, or I can just strangle you here. Your choice."

The pepper spray had sealed my eyes shut, and the rope was digging into me. I got up and shuffled forward as she pulled, trying to think of a way out.

Sue talked at me as we walked. "I thought you'd at least appreciate the use of poison and a rope since you have that ridiculous gaming idea for the house. Anyway, I hoped Trace would come to me for advice, but she just kept going to you. You are in my way. Trace and I are family, but you keep confusing things. Did you do anything when that animal went after her at the diner? No, I took care of that. I even made things better at her apartment for her. What have you done?" She snarled at me.

"You're right. You're much better for Trace than I could ever be. I'll tell Trace she can't stay here with me." I tried to sound sincere through the pain. "I'll tell Trace she needs to head back. I had no idea I was in your way." I was trying to stall and figure out a way to get away from her and closer to people. My emergency whistle was in my backpack. If I could get her backed off for a moment to grab it, someone might hear me. My head was pounding, and I had to keep wiping the tears away. The world tilted, and I fell back down as she yanked on the rope. Baron whined to my left.

"No, it won't work. You have to be gone. She'll grieve, but I'll be there for her. I'll help her through it as a true friend should. This is the best thing for us all."

Just then, Trace's phone went off in my pocket. "Wait, that will be a call for Trace. She's on call for emergency foster cat placements today and will be pretty ticked off at whoever kept her from getting the call."

"Well, you're useless so I guess I'd better get it for her. Then she'll know who her true friend is." I felt the rope loosen as she came towards me.

Bad enough that I had to walk into this mess, but I was done being insulted. I took off my backpack and swung it in her direction to try and knock her down. I twisted a little as the bag swung without impact. Then, all I felt was the rope tighten against the whistle around my neck.

Chapter Twenty-Eight

The quilt I was wrapped in seemed familiar, but the room, which looked alarmingly like a hospital room, made me worry. I was surrounded by four sets of blurry faces. I squinted at the bright light and tried to focus on at least one face.

"Wow, you look terrible," I said to Trace. Her hair was in a disheveled ponytail, there was no makeup, and she was wearing a wrinkled shirt.

"Remi! Thank heavens." Trace started to sit down on the bed but stopped herself. "The doctor left some stuff for the pain. Are you hurting? What can I get you? Do you want some water?"

I tried to wave my hand at her to get her to stop so I could get a word in edgewise or for her to at least stop screaming, but my hand was bandaged and currently occupied by a taped-up syringe.

I grimaced as I moved my head to try and see who else was there. Jason and Alice grinned with relief, and I was surprised to see Nick hovering in the background.

"Are you comfortable, dear?" asked Alice. "I brought this quilt from the inn because those hospital blankets are not as cozy."

I tried to smile, but that hurt my face. Slowly, the reason I was lying there came back, and I tried to rise out of bed.

"Where's Sue?" was closely followed by "ow, ow, ow," as I tried to talk with the swelling and bruising on my face made itself known. Trace and Alice gently laid me back down and helped me raise my head using the buttons on the bed.

I tried to grab Trace's hand. "She was waiting for me at the house. She's nuts."

"We know." Nick's voice came from my left, and I gently turned my head that way. "She's in police custody. She proudly told them her whole story while trying to convince them they needed to let her go so she could stay by Trace and be there for her while she grieved."

"Oh, yes, they should let her come by and be here for me," Trace said, her voice stone cold.

"Where's Baron?" I asked, my brain jumping from one thing to the next. I felt like I was a season behind on my favorite TV show and needed all the recap info as quickly as possible.

Jason spoke up. "Jake's dog sitting back at the inn. We did try to get him smuggled in, but he was a bit large."

I had a momentary image of them smuggling Jake into the hospital until I realized they meant Baron. Must be some good pain meds the doctors have me on. "This is a lot to take in, and my head hurts." Knowing that the psycho and my dog were both where they belonged, so many questions popped into my head. "I'm sorry, Trace. I should have realized it as Sue much sooner. Not much of a detective, huh? Have we found out what caused her to do all this craziness?" I took a sip of water and gave myself a pass on the bit that dribbled down my chin. Trace smiled and dabbed it for me.

"You won't believe it. Sue works at that movie theater in the shopping center next to my apartment complex. You know, the one I go to for their budget Tuesdays?"

I nodded carefully, wincing slightly from the ache while waiting for her to continue. Trace usually went to see the old movies for the two-dollar special.

"Anyway, Sue was one of the servers there, and in her head, she took it to think we had formed a bond. I never even noticed it was the same person that served me no matter where I sat." Trace took a sip out of my water cup. "It's not like you can even see the person, ya know? She'd been at the café and other places, but never got close to me. When Sue showed up here, I didn't recognize her."

She carefully sat on the edge of my bed. "She had even started following me home."

Nick chimed in. "Sheriff Marrow got permission to go into her house and he found a bunch of Trace's stuff, including her bike."

Trace shuddered.

"Sue had a whole shrine to Trace on her bedroom wall of photoshopped pictures of her and Sue spending time together. Best

Friends Forever was written above the photos. Strangely enough, you didn't make it into any of them." Nick said the last part as he leaned in conspiratorially to me.

Jason agreed. "From what we heard, your presence in any picture was violently removed. They were similar to what they found in Trace's neighbors. She killed him and set it up for him to take the fall as the stalker. Total whack job."

"So she just happened to be a letterboxer and a stalker?" I asked.

"She heard us talking about it and started up. Once she was more like you I would be wooed over to the dark side."

I closed my swollen eyes, letting my brain rest for a moment.

"How did you guys find me?"

Jason cleared his throat. "I was up on the roof getting ready to head in from my overnight watching when I saw you head into the wood path. I waved at you but realized you were too far away to see or hear me. I didn't want to yell any louder since the campers were below me, and it was pretty early. I was worried about you going off on your own with everything Alice had filled me in on, so I watched you. You'd turned because there was someone else there. Then I saw someone step out from behind the tree, and you both disappeared from sight." He took his cap off and smoothed his hair back. "I just thought you had met up with someone and gone off for a morning hike or something," a slight blush tinged his cheeks. "I should have known something was wrong." He looked away from me.

"There was no way you could know." I tried to reassure him.

"Anyway, a little bit later," Jason continued. "Sue came out of the woods, but no sign of you. As soon as I saw it was her I called the Sheriff and swung by to wake up Trace on my way downstairs."

That made me smile. I could only imagine the sight that greeted Jason when she opened the door. I was worried about her. She looked deathly pale.

"Sue was in the kitchen acting as if everything was normal. I tried to play along and asked if she'd seen you, and she shrugged and said you'd decided it was best to head out and get back to work. She and Trace would handle everything." His mouth tightened, and he ground out the next part. "I tried to get more information, but she started raving about how everything would be so much better now that you were gone.

Trace took the story back up from there. "The Sheriff must have broken some speed limits because he walked into the kitchen the same time as me. Sue rushed me and pulled me into a bear hug. I pushed away from her, and she put her hands on her hips and chastised me for not appreciating all that she'd done for me."

"Things moved pretty quickly after that," Alice said, "Sue's spiraled and practically bragged about all that she had done to keep Trace happy and safe. Sheriff Marrow took her in but she wouldn't say where you were, and I wasn't going to wait. We all ran around the inn, banging on doors, asking for people to come out and help us search. We gathered all the letterboxers in the area where you were last seen, but there was no luck at first."

"I used the Find My Phone app and got us as far as the house. Baron was barking at the door." Her voice cracked a little. "She'd put you under the tent."

Trace moved my bangs a little out of my eyes. "You were, uh, pretty beat up," she said.

"Doc says the levels that were left in the tent would compound the concussion you have as far as disorientation and pain." Trace tried to joke, but there was still a bit of fear in her eyes, and she kept touching my arm as if to make sure I hadn't disappeared.

I gave her the sternest face I could manage. "This was not your fault. Don't even go there. The only person to blame for this is that psycho Sue."

She shrugged and nodded a little, but I could tell guilt lingered. Someone killed people and hurt others because they were obsessed with her.

"How is Bob?" I didn't have much more visit left in me and needed to wrap it up.

She scowled. "He came through without a scratch. Sue had invited him down to the lake, and the next thing he knew was a sharp hit to the head and then waking up in the hospital. Thankfully, Sue's attempt at covering for herself by pretending to save him actually saved him."

"Saved him from her, at least," I said, remembering my chat with Nathan.

Bob knocked on the doorframe and stuck his head in. "Mind if I come in?-"

Everyone looked from him to me, and I nodded in agreement. They left to give us some space. I couldn't wait to hear this one.

He handed me the latest book in a series I loved. "I, uh, know you're not a fan of getting flowers, so I thought you'd like this instead." He paced around the room a bit. "Look, I know I've not handled things with you well, but it scared me how fast we were going, and I went ahead and sabotaged it and then freaked out that I ruined things. I handled the repair work just as badly."

I stayed quiet. A few days ago I would have taken this as the most personal discussion he'd ever had with me. I wasn't expecting a heartfelt chat. Now, it was step five in conning Remi out of her inheritance.

"When we found you hurt, I knew it was time to stop hiding and deal with things." He stopped beside the bed and put both hands on the railing as if to steady himself. "I don't expect you to trust me until I earn it, but I need to know if there's a chance."

He stood there, not speaking, and there was a tiniest echo in me reminding me of our good times. We had a lot of history together. But my head was screaming at me. This was another level to his manipulations, and I would be opening myself up to more emotional roller coasters. Even if there was a glimmer of truth to it, there was so much to our baggage now I would never be able to trust him in any deeper way. He must have seen the answer in my expression because he grimaced and nodded. "I get it. But I'm not going to give up, either. No more stalker, tent borrowing, jealousy-inducing games. Just me showing you that I can grow up."

He leaned down and kissed the side of my head without the bandage. "And if that means all we'll ever be to each other as friends, then I will be there for you as a friend."

Trace popped in and took up a spot between me and Bob, her arms crossed. "Aren't you forgetting something?" she asked. "We had a great chat with Nathan earlier about his real estate development firm and all of the plans you had for Remi's house."

I caught a quick look of surprise before he looked back at me. "We can talk about things when you're feeling better." He said. "We'd make a huge profit starting year one." He reached for my hand.

"Out. Get out. Be sure you're nowhere around when I get out." I said, drained of all emotion.

Nick waited for him to leave before coming back in. "I didn't know what to get someone for a concussion, but Alice mentioned you liked these, so..." He placed a small box of chocolate-covered strawberries in front of me.

"Yum! There are only four, though. None for you?" I teased.

"I wish I could stay and keep you company, but I have work in the morning, and I'm heading home in a bit. I didn't want to leave until I knew you were up and about first."

"So, where is home?" I asked, trying to be nonchalant and not like someone who wanted to track his car.

"According to Trace, and I have no reason to doubt her as she mapped it out for me, it's thirty-two minutes from your new place."

"She's very subtle." I smiled.

"So, I told her there is a Thai place by you that I strongly recommend for their Wednesday night specials." He grinned at me, his eyes twinkling with his smile.

"Hmm...I tend to eat dinner around six. Does it get crowded?"

He took my hand briefly. "I'll save you a spot when you're ready. Bring a card game to teach me."

We laughed as the others filtered back into the room with us.

"Any good news to share?" I asked.

"Chris solved the Golden Duck." Alice shared. "I had given everyone clues to find a certain portrait in the house. The alien portraits were kind of a clue as well to say you were looking for a painting. Specifically, the one in the foyer. It's of an old farmhouse and diesel truck. It's surrounded by crops with some laundry on the wire and a group of crows."

"It's good to see everyone in such high spirits." Sheriff Marrow stepped in and tipped his chin in my direction. "Ma'am, happy to see you awake. You can all rest easy and shouldn't have any more problems. However, you will all need to come back to testify. I don't want there to be any holes in this case." He said

"Of course. I'll be a local soon, so I'll be easy to find." Trace said.

He smiled. "Yes, ma'am. I'll be sure to mark that down. But first," he held up a necklace for her to see.

"My necklace!" Trace moved to reach for it.

Sheriff Marrow handed it to her. "Sue admits to stealing it, hiding it on Bob, and then grabbing it back before it got into evidence. Given the sentimentality of the necklace, we decided it was okay to give it back to you now. She even has a selfie on her phone of her wearing it. Proving she had it will not be difficult."

Trace closed her eyes and and took a deep breath. "Thank you." She said wasting no time in putting it back on.

"To finish up," Trace said. "Sue tried to convince the police..." She motioned to the Sheriff. "...that you attacked her, and she was just defending herself. She turned to me for support. Can you believe the nerve of that..." She took a calming breath. "Anyway, the police took her off. Finally knowing who we were after, they found Sue had two restraining orders against her and several other complaints from past friends and boyfriends. Your downfall was getting me to move here."

"Oh, well, in that case, the invite is canceled. Pack up," I joked.

"Sorry, I already have my room picked out. You're stuck with me." She went to fist bump me and changed it to a hand squeeze. . and caused a pain wince.

"Anywho, this is her first physical attack that they know of, so the police are going to want to take your statement as soon as you're up and ready. She's a third-time stalking offender and breaking probation. Another charge against her should put her away for about five years."

I closed my eyes for a moment, taking it all in. My energy level was depleted, and the people pounding hammers in my head weren't letting up. "Trace, could you see if you could get some volunteers to pick up the stamps? I don't want to go out for a bit."

Trace nodded. "Alice and I still need to find some, so we'll take care of it. You concentrate on feeling better."

"We'll do that, hon," Alice said. "Now, I know you're in a rush to get into your place, but it's gonna take a bit of labor to clean the place up. You don't need to do that for the next few days. You two will stay with us, and we'll help clean up."

I started to protest, and Alice cut me off.

"Don't be silly. Taking care of family comes first. You concentrate on getting better."

I blinked a little, and Trace handed me a tissue to blot my eyes.

"Well, I can't turn that down! Thank you. Both of you have been wonderful. Wow, looks like everything's solved except for the aliens. Got any news on that front for me, Jason?"

"Reports are saying it was some "swamp gas." Do you see a swamp near here?" He gestured out the window to the forest. "Some are saying weather balloons and a few are going with the stray meteors theory. I couldn't find anything that would show a landing or even a visitation. Charlie and Chuck are both ranting all over town. They're convinced it's a government coverup and are demanding to talk to someone about where the aliens are being kept." He chuckled.

"You don't seem heartbroken about it. Got a secret UFO secreted away on the farm somewhere?"

Alice rolled her eyes but gave her husband a one-armed hug. "That's because with all the binoculars and telescopes running rampant the past few days, there were new reports about Clyde."

"Clyde?" Trace, Nick, and I all asked at once.

"The local lake monster," Sheriff Marrow provided. "I'm guessing you haven't gone through much of the things in the house yet?"

"I'm not sure I want to ask how that's related to Clyde?"

He chuckled. "Rumor has it your aunt Rosemary was quite the Clyde hunter."

"Maybe that's what happened to the missing husband." We laughed a little, but laughing was not on my happy head list, and it turned to "Ow, ow, ow, ow."

Jason patted my non-syringed arm. "You rest for now. Doc will discharge you today as long as you come back to the inn under our watchful care."

"There's lasagna for dinner," Alice offered.

Trace hugged me carefully and opened the hospital door to leave, but people crowding the door forced her to shut it again. Voices on the other side called my name. "Do you care to leave a statement, Ms. McKenna?" one of the voices shouted through the door's industrial glass window.

"You're the biggest news we've had in this area since a movie was filmed here a few years ago. They want to know if you're keeping the Kerr place after everything."

Of course, I was keeping it. The beautiful, permitless, bug-infested place was mine! My plans, hopes, and dreams could finally be realized. Alice squeezed my hand, and I realized I had been lost in my thoughts.

I grinned, ignoring the pain. "Let them know it will be a premier board game cafe. I already have the name. Meeple Manor."

About the author

Shelley Shearer always wanted to be a ninja or an astronaut or zoologist. So now she spends her time dabbling in as many adventures as she can manage. Snuggling lemurs, experiencing zero gravity, attending police seminars and mounted archery are some of the ways she tries to keep her life as interesting as the ones she writes about. Shelley writes both urban fantasy and mystery and has short stories in the Black Market Anthology, Chesapeake Crimes 3, and Chesapeake Crimes: They Had It Comin'.

f facebook.com/shellshearerwriter

Made in the USA
Middletown, DE
09 March 2024

50566340R00119